📁 To JayKae:
LIFE STINX

By Jean Davies Okimoto

NOVELS

My Mother Is Not Married to My Father
It's Just Too Much
Norman Schnurman, Average Person
Who Did It, Jenny Lake?
Jason's Women
Molly by Any Other Name
Take a Chance, Gramps!
Talent Night
The Eclipse of Moonbeam Dawson
To Jaykae: Life Stinx

PICTURE BOOKS

Blumpoe the Grumpoe Meets Arnold the Cat
A Place for Grace
No Dear, Not Here

SHORT STORIES

"Jason the Quick and the Brave"
"Moonbeam Dawson and the Killer Bear"
"Next Month . . . Hollywood!"
"Watching Fran"
"Eva and the Mayor"

PLAYS

Hum It Again, Jeremy
Uncle Hideki

NONFICTION, COAUTHOR

Boomerang Kids: How to Live with
Adult Children Who Return Home

To JayKae:
LIFE STINX

Jean Davies Okimoto

A Tom Doherty Associates Book
NEW YORK

TO JAYKAE: LIFE STINX

This book is printed on acid-free paper.

A Tor Book
Published by Tom Doherty Associates, LLC
175 Fifth Avenue
New York, NY 10010

www.tor.com

Tor® is a registered trademark of Tom Doherty Associates, LLC.

Design by Lisa Pifher

Library of Congress Cataloging-in-Publication Data

Okimoto, Jean Davies.
    To Jaykae : life stinx / Jean Davies Okimoto. — 1st ed.
        p.   cm.
    "A Tom Doherty Associates book."
    Sequel to: Jason's women.
    Summary: Sixteen-year-old Jason feels alone and misunderstood when his best friend moves away, his father plans to remarry, and his step-brother-to-be is a high school basketball star, until he starts an on-line relationship with a girl from Hawaii.
    ISBN 0-312-86732-8
    [1. Remarriage Fiction.   2. Electronic mail messages Fiction.   3. Interpersonal relations Fiction.   4. High schools Fiction.   5. Schools Fiction.]   I. Title.
    PZ7.O415To   1999
    [Fic]—dc21

Fic
Oki
c 2

99-38398
CIP

Printed in the United States of America

0 9 8 7 6 5 4 3

For Margy

📂 To JayKae:
LIFE STINX

One

WHEN BERTHA JANE DIED it was like the sun died. It was dark even on the brightest days. And Thao, the only person I knew who missed her the way I did, had gone, too. Beautiful Thao, she left just a few weeks later. Not only is Thao one of the strongest people I ever met, but she is so beautiful it could break your heart. And I think it came close to breaking mine when she left.

Thao Nguyen was like my sister. Not that I hadn't wanted it to be more than that, I did, I wanted a lot more. But there were circumstances beyond my control, such as the small fact that I am not Vietnamese, which made a relationship between me and Thao impossible. Impossible according to her family. My family (if you could call us that) is a bit different. My parents are divorced and wouldn't care if I got involved with a recently paroled murderess as long as I didn't bother them.

When I was hit over the head with the reality that there was no hope for me and Thao, Bertha Jane tried to console me. She reminded me that we could still be friends and that this was a very big deal. In fact, Bertha Jane thought friendship was one of the most important things on earth. She thought it mattered more than anything, even sex. And I have to admit, it was kind of weird talking to this old lady about sex. Bertha Jane was eighty-three when she died, and even now I can hear her whispery voice when we had that conversation: "I'm not against sex, Jason, but sometimes when things are felt with lust and passion, true friendship can be obscured."

It took me a long time to appreciate that. Sex was pretty high on my list. Not that I was having any, but sex for me was like winning the lottery, something I dreamed about all the time. To be honest, I still do, but what happened between Thao and Bertha Jane and me was like finding gold. We became family. And now Bertha Jane is in heaven (if there is such a place, she's there, believe me) and Thao thinks she's landed in hell. Right after Bertha Jane died, she moved to California.

I met Bertha Jane through a help-wanted ad in the newspaper, and Thao lived with her. Bertha Jane had sponsored Thao to come to America from Vietnam. It ended up that I was the help that Bertha Jane wanted. She hired me to be what she called a jack-of-all-trades and I loved that job. There wasn't a day that I didn't look forward to going to work. I was supposed to tutor Thao in English, which was a joke since Thao ended up helping me (with my life) more than I helped her with English. I also drove Bertha Jane places, did gardening, odd jobs, and worked on Bertha Jane's campaign for mayor. One of the last things Bertha Jane did before she died was mount a political campaign so she could have a forum for her philosophy and her ideas about how the world could be better.

Bertha Jane died four months ago and I still haven't found another job. I don't feel like looking for one, either. In fact, I don't feel like doing anything. For example, getting out of bed: When I'm not at school, I am basically spending my life between the sheets. So far my dad hasn't said anything about this. Oh, there's been the occasional abbreviated spin of his standard motivational lecture, but it's more like he's humming the first few bars of rousing marching music and it fades away when he sees that I am tone-deaf. To give him a little credit, I'd have to say even though he never knew either Bertha Jane or Thao, he actually does seem to understand that something sad happened to me. Although it's probably in some abstract way, like most things with my dad, he doesn't really get it. My dog, Fred, seems to understand more than my dad. He always sleeps on my bed and there is a way he acts that just gives me the sense that he knows. I'm not sure how to explain this, but it just feels that way. Fred *knows*. But as far as my dad goes, I admit I'm grateful that at least he hasn't been on my case in any major way.

That is until now.

Today when I got home from school there was a voice-mail message that sounded like the stuff was about to hit the fan.

"Jason, this is Dad. Be home tonight. I've got to talk to you, be there at six."

Clunk. He just hangs up.

On a good day, Dad is not exactly Mr. Manners, but this message went beyond his usual bark. My dad is a big, burly guy (beefy arms, hairy chest; sort of a John Belushi type if he'd lived to be Dad's age) and very different from me. I'm always stuffing my face with food and working out with weights, but I still have the build of a noodle. Dad thinks I'm a noodle, too. Oh man, I hope he doesn't want me home tonight for a full dose of the Beasley Motivation Seminar. I hate that crap. Dad went to this seminar about six months ago, and it was like he had found a religion.

He has special books and tapes and videos that focus on the Beasley Motivation method and believe me, these teaching materials cost an arm and a leg. I think the person who got motivated to develop his full potential (to get rich) was Chester P. Beasley, founder. My dad is always spouting off the stuff they teach and trying to convert everyone, especially me. He goes back to the Beasley Motivation Seminar for refresher courses and gets totally psyched. I could care less, except when he gets pumped up to do something about my life.

Dad has always thought I had no motivation to do anything.

It's true now, but it wasn't true when Bertha Jane was alive and Thao was here. There were a number of things I was motivated about, like sex for example. And birds. I'm not a serious birder, out in the bushes with a bird book and binoculars, but I like birds. I like to feed them, ordinary birds, like sparrows and pigeons and seagulls. I feed them because they're hungry. I also like watching Canada geese. A lot of people hate them because their crap is as big as a cocker spaniel's and it's everywhere. There are a lot of parks where you wouldn't want to slide into base because of goose poo, but I like them anyway. It amazes me how they get into such a nice V shape and fly around like that. And how do they choose which goose is going to be the head guy, or lady, for that matter? Ha! Maybe it's Mother Goose. Actually, I'm still motivated to watch Canada geese, but Dad wouldn't understand that. But I admit I'm not motivated to do much else, and so what? Go motivate yourself, Bozo, is what I say to that.

Dad's wasn't the only message on the voice mail. There was one from Kenny Newman.

"Hey, Kovak, I got two Sonics tickets from my uncle. Call me if you want to go. If I don't get a call by five I'll start calling around. Bye."

It was four fifty-five. I had five minutes.

I like the Sonics a lot. I don't love them the way I love the Mariners, but I'd still go to a Sonics game any time I had the chance. Actually, sports was something else Bertha Jane and I had in common. Not just sports, but specifically baseball. She loved the Mariners, which I thought was unusual for someone her age. She knew the names of all the players, even all the batting averages. She didn't actually attend the games; watching them on TV was her thing. But she always fixed herself a hot dog and had a beer or two and sat there like she was in the stands. She would clap and cheer at that TV like they could hear her. Bertha Jane said she liked baseball better than basketball because there were more kinds of people. It didn't have anything to do with the nature of the game, really. Just the people who played the game. "Jason, in basketball, for the most part you, just have two colors of people. Black and white. But in baseball you have black and white, but then you have a lot of brown people, and even that fellow for the Yankees, from Japan, another color there, too. It's much more interesting."

And she had hope. She never gave up on them even when they were on a big losing streak. Even when they were totally trounced, playing like pathetic losers, she'd find something good to say about someone on the team. Bertha Jane had enthusiasm for things. Not just baseball, but all kinds of things, like when the first crocus peeped up in her yard, she would be thrilled like it was the most exciting thing that had ever happened. I keep trying to accept that she had a long life, but as hard as I try to really get this, I still feel that Bertha Jane was someone who just shouldn't have died. I know it doesn't make sense, but that's how I feel about it.

Even though I don't love the Sonics the way I love the Mariners, I definitely wanted to go to the game with Kenny. Why couldn't Dad just as easily talk to me after the game? After all, most of the time he doesn't care if I'm here or not. But as I reach for the phone to call Kenny, an argument starts in my head.

"*Dad's going to be pissed when he gets home and you're not here.*"

"So? I'll just say I never picked up the message."

"*Maybe he's coming home to tell you he has cancer.*"

"Ever since Bertha Jane died you think everyone has cancer! We're playing the Bulls, jerkhead."

"*Maybe his company went belly-up and you have to move.*"

"Fine. I'll move to California and I can see Thao. Just shut up, already!"

That voice ended the argument and I went ahead and called. Kenny answered on the first ring.

"Hey, man, thanks for calling about the tickets. I'm on."

"It's good you called, I was about to try Keo."

"Yeah, glad I caught you. Want me to drive?"

"No problem. I got my dad's car. Pick you up at five-thirty."

There was another reason I jumped at the chance to go with Kenny. He was between women and I knew it wouldn't be that long before he was involved again and spending every minute with a new lady. It was getting predictable. Kenny and I had been friends since we were little kids, but last year everything changed. We were still good friends; in fact, probably Kenny would still say I was his best friend, but there was something new in the equation. Girls. All of a sudden our sophomore year they just loved the guy. I have tried to figure this out. In fact, I have spent hours thinking about it because I would like to get this to happen to me. But I still don't know what Kenny does to get girls the way he does. He's had somebody all last year and this year, too. Last year he went with Sarah Klein who is in my homeroom. She's incredible. I can't remember why they broke up, but then second semester he gets involved with Nina Brim. Also incredible. Then she leaves for the summer and he has a big summer romance with Naomi Brim, Nina's sister. That got pretty intense, but then they break up and he starts going with Kimberly Cotton. But they broke up last week. I don't know all the details yet, but it was no surprise when he called me about the Sonics tickets. If he was still with her, believe me, she'd be going to the game tonight and not me. Last year this kind of thing pissed me off, but now I've finally accepted that's how it is with Kenny.

While I waited for Kenny, I thought about Kimberly Cotton. She is a very cute sophomore and her looks and personality, everything about her seems like her name, fluffy and soft. I wondered what would happen if I tried to get something going with her. After all, her relationship with Kenny was over. Then I hear that voice again, and the other one, too.

"Kimberly Cotton? Visit reality."

"Shut up. I got so I could talk to girls 'cause of Thao."

"That was Thao. She's different and you know it."

"She's female. And I talked to her all the time, it was easy with Thao. I even asked her out."

"Yeah, and it blew up in your face. Kimberly Cotton? Sure. You're out of your friggin' mind."

I got sick of these voices so I went to my room to check my E-mail before Kenny came. I got my own computer when my parents split up, a guilt gift. Mom paid for the computer and Dad bought a printer, a bunch of software and games, and a year's worth of America Online. But if I go over the monthly fee I'm supposed to pay. I've found many interesting Web sites, but I don't have a credit card so I can't get too far. I know Dad never thought I was on the Net doing research for homework; he thinks I'm playing video games and stuff. And if he knows I've been checking out the sex sites he hasn't said anything. Actually, when I'm not asleep I am always checking out the free pics on the trial offers.

Maybe that's it. Maybe Dad's mad because the AOL bill is getting big and I don't have a job yet to pay him back. I had offered to give him the money Mom gave me for my birthday and Christmas, but he said to keep it for stuff I wanted and pay him when I got a job (I don't think he realized how far I can make money go). But if the conversation is about money, I just hope he doesn't try to motivate me with the Beasley Motivation Seminar. I know his whole speech by heart, so he might as well save his breath.

"Jason," he says, "you've got to go for it! If you see something you want in this world, you've got to go for it." Then he reaches in his wallet and whips out his business card. Then he points at it and he says, "Now see this card here? It used to embarrass your mother, but she wasn't too embarrassed to spend the profits, I'll tell you that."

Then he jabs the card some more with his finger. "This card, this card here represents going for it. And that's what you've got to do now. You've got to get out there and go for it!"

Then he holds the card like he was holding an original copy of the Declaration of Independence and says solemnly, "Kovak Kans."

Then he winks. "Cans spelled with a *K,* a cute little marketing thing there." Then he reads, this time like he's announcing the winner of the Academy Awards. "Jack Kovak, Colonel of the Urinal!"

Then he pauses and says, "Now a lot of people might think Colonel of the Urinal is a silly slogan. But I'll tell you, they never forget it. We outsell Sanikans and Johnny-on-the-Spot two to one! And you know what, Jason?"

This is where I'm supposed to say, "What?" (like I never heard this crap before). And he says, "It all happened when I went to the Beasley Motivation Seminar for entrepreneurs and small-business executives. The slogan just popped into my head like a gift . . . Colonel of the Urinal! As soon as I used this slogan, Kovak Kans took off like nobody's business. I say affirmations I learned at the seminar every morning. And I want you to start doing it, too."

Then he says, "All you do is stand in front of the mirror and look yourself in the eye and say, "I am capable and competent. I am a winner. Today, I will be all I can be."

Then he tries to get me to say it after him. This is where I leave. I don't tell him that Chester P. Beasley has all the originality of an army commercial. I just leave and tell him I'll try it myself on my own. This is where I go in the bathroom and look in the mirror and say solemnly, "My dad is a nutcase."

I heard Kenny honk. I grabbed my fleece jacket and ran out to the drive. His dad's car is an Acura, very cool. I didn't blame him for not wanting to go in my beater; it's an old Ford. F.a.r.d. That's what my dad calls it, "Fix-And-Repair-Daily." Sometimes I've thought about getting one of those bumper stickers that says BEATS WALKING. Actually, I saw two stickers the other day I also liked a lot on an old Chevy. To the left of the license plate was CREATE RANDOM AND SENSELESS ACTS and on the other side: VISUALIZE WHIRLED PEAS.

I started saving up for my car as soon as I got my work permit when I was fifteen. That's when I went to work at Wendy's. My mom and dad chipped in to help me get that car, which was right around the time Mom moved out. Guilt seems to be quite a good motivator, I wonder if Chester P. Beasley is aware of that.

I left the house and locked the door behind me. Kenny was parked in the drive with the engine running. His dad's Acura is black, very sharp. I jumped in, slammed the door, took my shades out of my pocket, and put them on. I admit I was trying to look cool, since it was close to six and the sun was starting to go down. Next to Kenny I am sort of an immature person. Not that I'm a hairless pip-squeak with a girl voice. I shave, I have a low voice. (Okay, once in awhile when I'm nervous it cracks, but that hardly happens anymore.) And I'm about the same height as Kenny, 5' 10". But I still feel younger than Kenny. It's a mental thing.

All the way to the game he talked about Kimberly Cotton and how stupid it was that she had gotten so pissed just 'cause he had his arm around Rhondelle Jackson, which is I guess why they broke up.

"Girls melt down sometimes over nothing."

"Yeah." I nodded, shoving my shades back (they'd slipped down on my nose). "Over dumb stuff."

"I mean, it wasn't like I was hittin' on her."

"No way," I agreed, as if I'd been there.

" 'Cause when I hit on someone, they sure as hell know it!" Kenny looked over at me, grinning. "Right, man?"

"Right!" I grinned back at him like I knew what it was to be hittin' on someone.

I'm not sure what Kenny thinks—he saw me at school with Thao before she moved and asked me about her. He said we looked pretty tight and complimented me on my good taste in women. He said she was gorgeous (which she is). It was fine with me if he wanted to think it was physical, because this is not lying to the guy. This is just letting him make assumptions. He can make all the assumptions he wants as far as I am concerned. I like assumptions about me and Thao.

Then we passed the new baseball stadium and Kenny started talking about the Mariners and how great it was in the old days when they had the big unit, Randy Johnson. This was a better conversation as far as I was concerned because the hitting I could talk about was something I knew about: baseball.

But the Sonics were great. It was fun being there with Kenny and I found myself hoping he wouldn't get a new girlfriend for a while. I know that's selfish, but that's what I was thinking. Either that or I would get one and then we could do a lot of stuff together, Kenny, his new girlfriend and me and mine. And I began to wonder if things really were over between him and Kimberly, if he'd mind if I got something going with her.

On the way home from the game, I was starting to have the same Kimberly conversation in my head again, but I quit thinking about her when we pulled up in front of my house. All the lights were on downstairs. Usually houses that are lit up on a dark street look friendly and inviting, but the lights in my house meant Dad was home and I would be invited in for a big hassle, and it would not be friendly. There was no getting around it. When he left the message telling me to be home at six it was unusual. And his tone had been serious when he told me he wanted to talk to me. And what did I do? Blew him off, that's what, I admit it. So right now getting in my car and driving anywhere was a lot more appealing than going in the house. It's not that I'm afraid of my dad (okay, maybe a little) but it's left over from when I was younger and I got scared when he yelled. Now what I can't stand, what I really *hate*, is being hassled. Another argument begins in my head:

"I gotta think of something so I don't have to go in there."

"Don't worry. Be happy."

"Very funny."

"Maybe what he wants to talk about isn't a big deal."

"Maybe the Easter bunny will come down the chimney."

"Okay, but if he does blow up 'cause you weren't home at six he'll get over it in a day or two."

"Sure."

"You know he's like that. He blows up but then he gets over it."

That thought was a little convincing. He usually does get over being mad after a few days. Reminding myself of this fact helped give me enough nerve to go in the house. But believe me, I was not going in there banging like a sonic boom.

I tiptoed.

Slowly, I go up to the door on the super power-reinforced toes of my Nikes.

Carefully, I slide the key in the lock like a burglar cracking a safe that is wired with explosives.

Then, trying not to breath, I inch the door open and turn to shut it behind me, hoping it will close without a click. But Dad must have heard Kenny's car, because just as I get the door shut, he storms into the kitchen. He hovers there, a giant hulk blocking the stairs to the basement.

"Where've you been!"

"Sonics game." An innocent grin breaks across my face. "They beat the Bulls!"

"I told you to be here at six, Jason!" Dad yells, then he glances toward the den and lowers his voice to a growl. "I was very clear about it."

"I didn't even see you this morning." A puzzled look crosses my brow.

"I left the message on the voice mail," he snarls.

"Oh. Well, I . . ." I choke a little here.

"Don't lie to me! I know you got it, because it was erased when I got home!"

"I must have erased it by mistake," I mumble.

Dad looked like he was about to explode, but then he glanced toward the den again, trying to get control of himself. "Okay, well, come in the den now, so we can talk to you."

"We?" I am clueless. Who is "we"? But I am trapped, so I follow him. There is no way out of this.

The lamp on the hall table glows, and as he crosses in front of the light, my father's shadow looms large on the wall behind it like a giant ape. I walk behind him looking at the pattern in the carpet, wishing I were Air Jordan and I could leap over him and bound out of the house.

"Hi, Jason!" A pudgy lady pops out of the den with a big grin on her face. She is my dad's girlfriend, Doreen Kemple. Her hair is blond and pouffy and her face kind of pink. She is wearing a royal blue blouse and matching silk pants and a lot of gold jewelry that looks like the stuff on the shopping channel. There is something about her that reminds me of Miss Piggy.

"Hi." I attempted a polite smile, thinking about Kermit the Frog.

Dad and Doreen went in the den and I stayed in the doorway and leaned against the doorjamb. I thought about chewing tobacco and why it would be good to have a big wad of it right now. I've never actually chewed, but for some reason that's what I wished I had. A great big wad puffing out of my cheek and then I'd have to go outside and spit.

"Sit down, Jason." Dad and Doreen sat on the brown leather couch across from the TV. So I sat in the small wooden chair next to the door. It had a red pillow with designs on it that Mom picked up at some antique place. It was so pretty, I always thought it wasn't quite right to sit on it.

"Jason." Dad paused and looked at Doreen, then turned back to me. He swallowed, and I saw his Adam's apple bob up and down. Then in a nice voice he said, "Jason, the news we have is that Doreen is going to be your stepmother. We've decided to get married."

They both sat there grinning at me, waiting for me to say something. Dad's Adam's apple bobbed some more, and Doreen licked her lips and grinned. They stared at me, waiting. Waiting I suppose for "Congratulations," or "That's great!" Waiting for something positive and friendly.

But I felt like I hadn't quite heard. Don't get me wrong, I really *had* heard him. I knew what he said, all right, he said he and Doreen were going to get married. But it wasn't computing. I never thought he would get married again, at least not for a long time. Maybe when I was out of college or thirty or something. My dad had been seeing Doreen for a while (he had hardly been home the past six months) but there had been a lot of women before Doreen. After Mom left he went out constantly, seems like everyone he knew—our neighbors, people from his work, everyone was trying to fix him up with some woman. It had been like the Dating Game around here. I guess I hadn't noticed that Doreen turned into the whole game.

"Jason?" Dad looked at me, waiting for me to say something.

"Oh." That's all I could think of to say. Dad kept waiting for more, but my brain was stuck. If I had been chewing this would have been another good moment to go out and spit.

"So Jason? What do you say?" Dad leans forward on the couch, ready to hang on my every word.

I look at him and Doreen, and for a minute it is like an out-of-body experience and it feels as if I am on the ceiling gazing down at my dad and this woman in royal blue who looks like Miss Piggy who are both staring at me. Finally I think of something to say.

"Oh. You're getting married." I mouth the words like a robot.

Doreen folded her hands in her lap, her gold bracelets jangling, and leaned forward. "Jason, we had started to talk about getting married this coming summer, but we've had to speed it up a bit."

I am back on the ceiling looking down. Looking at her stomach. *Jeez, don't tell me she's pregnant.* I guess anything's possible these days, but she sure seems old. I stare at her, wondering what the hell is happening.

"My son, Josh, lives with his father in Chicago and his father's been transferred to Mexico City. Josh doesn't want to finish his senior year there so he's coming to live with me."

There is more silence and they look at me eagerly, wanting me to speak. But all I can do is repeat what I've heard. *I Am a Teenage Tape Recorder.* Like a machine I repeat, "So he's coming to live with—"

"Yes," she interrupts, talking so fast she reminds me of an auctioneer. "He's-visited-me-here-before-of-course. But-this-will-be-the-first-time-he'll-live-here." *Sold! To the teenage tape recorder, one pudgy lady with kid.*

"The first time he'll live here," I repeat. But then I got a little curious. "So why get married just 'cause he's moving in?"

Doreen started squirming, her silk pants swished around on the leather couch and she glanced at Dad. His Adam's apple bobbed up and down again as he swallowed several times. Then she said just as fast, "We spend a lot of time together and thought it'd be more comfortable for everyone if we were married."

"More comfortable?" I ask.

There is silence now, except for Doreen's pants swishing on the couch. Her bracelets jangle as she places her hand on Dad's arm and shoots him a look that is clearly intended to get him to speak, but he only swallows.

"Jack?"

Dad gets a sappy grin on his face. More swallowing.

She takes a deep breath, puffing up like a pigeon. "My condo only has one bedroom." The bracelets jangle as she begins to fidget with her fingernails.

Dad swallows again, but then speaks. "Doreen would have to get a new place anyway, so we just decided that she and Josh would move in here and we'd move up the wedding."

"Oh."

"You'll have a stepbrother, Jason. Won't that be great?"

"Josh is coming at the end of the week so he can start the semester here," Doreen chimed in.

"We're invited to her place Thursday night, so you can meet each other."

"Oh." I nodded. "So is that all?"

They looked at each other and both shrugged.

So I left.

Before I left, though, I took the red pillow. It would look better in my room than on that chair.

I went down to my room, threw the pillow on my bed, then opened my soft case, took out a CD, put it in my Discman, and stuck on my earphones. Then I flopped on my bed. Then I started to feel kind of sick, dizzy, and kind of weak.

I got up and went to the window and opened it. It was raining a little, but I stuck my head out anyway. I wished there was a moon. A big yellow moon with gray clouds rolling over it and I could howl at it. *Aowooooo . . . Aowoooooooo . . .*

The music was getting me depressed, so I went over to my dresser, opened my soft case again, and got another CD. While I was putting it in my Discman, I heard Dad call down to me.

"Jason! Come on up a minute will you?"

I stuck the earphones back in my ears, flopped on my bed again, and turned toward the wall. I lay there looking at the wall, moving my feet to the beat.

Then I felt a hand on my shoulder. I jumped like I hadn't been expecting it. Then I looked over at him and turned down the volume.

"Doreen and I are leaving. I'm going to take her back to her place. Come up and say good-bye."

I put the volume back up and turned toward the wall.

Big hand on my shoulder, shaking me. Then he yanks off my earphones.

"What the hell are you doing!"

"I said to come up and say good-bye." Dad glared at me.

"No."

"What d'ya mean, 'no'?"

"No."

"What the hell's wrong with you, Jason?"

"What the hell's wrong with *you*?"

He looks shocked. "Is this about Doreen and me?"

"I could care less."

"Well, if you don't care I'm getting married, then I don't get it."

"Exactly. Mom was right."

"What's that supposed to mean?"

"That you don't get it!"

"Fine. Why don't you tell me then." His jaw muscles twitch.

I looked away from him and stared at my Third Eye Blind poster.

"What was I supposed to say with *her* there?"

"You wanted me to ask your permission first, I suppose. Is that it?"

"It was a cheap shot because you don't give a sh—"

"Watch your language, Jason."

"Fine. You just wanted to make your little announcement and you had her there for cover so you wouldn't have to talk about it.

Just like when Mom left, so you wouldn't have to talk to me."

"I can see this isn't getting anywhere."

That's all he says. Then he leaves.

Then I lose it. Big time.

I'm crying like I'm five.

⌁ Two

THE REST OF THE NIGHT was strange. I was crying on and off and my stomach hurt. I kept going to the window and sticking my head out. It reminded me of how I felt when Mom and Dad first got divorced. That news made me quite sick until I finally faced the fact that not only was it going to happen, but that I was helpless to do anything about it.

Helpless, but not hopeless. I had high hopes back then, not the typical hope that they would stay together; my hope was more spectacular. I hoped they would have a huge custody fight. They would each want me so much they would have the biggest custody fight in the history of the state of Washington. It would go on for years. In and out of court, appeal after appeal . . . and the fight goes on! It would be featured on TV, a special on *You Be the Judge*. It would be so historic that *Frontline* would do a whole documentary on it. And, of course, over the years both of them would have tons of lawyers, the kind of expert lawyers they have on TV, armies of them carrying leather briefcases with shiny gold locks.

Throughout the fight, my mother would often be in hysterics, a complete meltdown. She would sob, "My boy! My boy! You can't take my boy!" And the judge who looked like Janet Reno would pound the gavel and say, "Order! Order in the court! Control yourself, Mrs. Kovak! Control yourself!"

But what actually happened was that Dad took me to Westport to go fishing and when we got back at the end of the weekend, Mom was gone. Some of the furniture was gone, too. Also the plants, most of the paintings and artsy stuff, a bunch of dishes, candlesticks, books, a few lamps—all gone. Whoosh! Vanished! Now you see them, now you don't.

The kitchen especially looked different, although I couldn't tell exactly what was missing. But I remember looking in her closet. I don't know why that got me, but when I saw that empty closet I lost it. Dad was out in the garage, which was just as well. The whole fishing trip he kept talking about all the stuff we were going to do, as if living without Mom was going to be a real picnic. Right. When I looked in that closet it was about as much fun as a picnic in a funeral home.

Dad hung with me for about a week and it turned out it was sort of fun. We rented videos, tried to cook, and also ate out a lot—usually at this great restaurant in the neighborhood, La Medusa. But after the week was up, someone at his work fixed him up with a date and from that moment on he went nuts. I quit trying to remember the names of all the women he went out with. He also bought a red Corvette. Seriously, that's what he did. Of course, I couldn't drive it, he didn't seem to even want me to ride in it much. I think having a teenage son took something away from his new image. It was bad enough having Mom gone, but when Dad disappeared into the dating game, I felt like everyone had jumped ship and now it was just me and Fred and we were going down with the rats. Luckily, it wasn't too long after Mom left that I met Bertha Jane and Thao.

I quit thinking about the divorce and stuck my head out the window and tried to stop crying, but the weird thing was that I didn't even know what it was about anymore. And then I hear Bertha

Jane. I don't understand this, but I looked up at the sky and the rain fell against my face and I was sitting beside her again in the hospital.

"Tears are put there for a reason, Jason. Like rain, they can't be stopped. And like rain, they help things grow."

She's here in some way that I can't explain, and her voice is strong within me, but it's not my words or my voice. It's unmistakably Bertha Jane, and my heart hears her soft voice.

"When we fully accept our sadness, marrow-deep in our bones, we grow beyond the idea that the purpose of life is constant pleasure."

I stopped crying and I pulled my head inside and closed the window. Then I lay down on my bed for a while. I feel surprisingly calm. It's so weird that I wonder if I get up again and stick my head out the window if I'll hear Bertha Jane's voice again, so I do it. I have to check this out.

I hop off the bed, go to the window, yank it open, and pop my head out.

I wait.

I wait some more. Listening.

I lean out farther and lift up my head, letting the rain fall all over my face.

Still no Bertha Jane.

So I close the window.

But even though I didn't hear her voice again, I keep feeling calm. It still seems like she's nearby. And I want to hold on to the closeness, so I lie back and Fred jumps up on the bed with me. He curls against my side with his head on my arm, and I actually feel pretty good, or at least not that bad anymore.

But as much as I want to keep this feeling, I can't. And after awhile, like a creek rising over its bank after a storm, reality washes over me: Dad won't be coming back. He'll spend the night at Doreen's and there's no one here but me and Fred. So I decide that even though Bertha Jane seems to be with me, it would be good to talk to someone who's not dead.

I grab the phone and call Kenny, but it just rings once and goes into voice mail, so I hang up. When it rings once like that, it means he's talking to someone. So I wait a couple of minutes and I call again. Kenny has voice mail and call waiting, so I figure if I'm persistent he might pick up. And the third time I call, it works. He answers right away.

"Hey, Kenny."

"I'm on the other line with Kimberly, Jason. I'll call you tomorrow."

Click.

"Fred, it's time for me to surf the Net." I give Fred a little pat and go to my computer. "They have lots of interesting things on the Internet," I explain to Fred.

I know, you're thinking I'm trying to cheer myself up by finding the sex on the Net. Maybe. But first, for the hell of it, I decide to see what's going on in a chat room. When the AOL Channels page comes up, I click on "People Connection," then on "Chat Now!" At the top of the screen it says, "You have just entered room 'Town Square—Lobby 43.' "

Usually, I just read what people are saying and I don't chat myself. And I usually get bored after a few minutes. Also, it seems like whenever I've been in a chat room, some jerk gets in the room and messes it up and they threaten to cut off his account. The screen name I use is JayKae, which I picked for my initials J. K. At first I wrote it "JayKay" but I thought it looked like a girl's name or a brand of plastic food containers like they have at Wal-Mart, so I changed the "Kay" to "Kae." A lot more cool, for sure. Tonight I sat there for a while just reading the conversation (if you could call it that). Like I said, I never chat, I just read.

Slimer45:	i understand that
Smilly2003:	HEY PEEPS SUP?
SKYLA70s:	hey
ITZSTUMPY:	where u from
Puff9292:	any cute guys in here?

Smilly2003:	boring ohio
TennisGA114:	13f anyone wanna talk
Slimer45:	Ohio sux right
Flownder02:	age sex check
LeeshaPunk:	11f
ITZSTUMPY:	duz ne 1 here believe in aliens?
CrAzY16308:	hey all, whatcha all doing?
Sarahbuddy:	i have a dog buddy and if you want me to tell you about him talk to me. He is really neat!
Flownder02:	no, u crazy
ITZSTUMPY:	hey, duz ne1 here believe in aliens?

This is about where I would get off, but then this girl got on. At least I hoped she was really a girl.

Surfsup10:	Hey n e 16 m's in here?
Sarahbuddy:	My dog really is cool.
Bryc06:	ANY GIRLS HAVE A PIC PRESS 235
Surfsup10:	n e 1 wanna talk with a 16/f
Flownder02:	ur a pervert, so's ur dog

I kept looking at Surfsup10 and then I don't know why, but I just jumped in.

JayKae:	Hey Surf, 16/m here
Surfsup10:	Cool. Where u from

Then we just started chatting in the middle of all the other people's junk. Here's what we said (without the other junk).

JayKae:	Seattle u?
Surfsup10:	Hawaii
JayKae:	Cool. Honolulu?
Surfsup10:	Maui. Been there?
JayKae:	In 7th grade, with the rents.

Surfsup10:	Think they'll take you again?
JayKae:	No. They're divorced.
Surfsup10:	Mine 2. It sux
JayKae:	Agree. My dad's getting married.
Surfsup10:	When?
JayKae:	Dunno. Just found out.
Surfsup10:	My mom remarried two years ago. What music u like?
JayKae:	Tupac. But old stuff 2. Beatles. Grateful Dead. Pink Floyd.
Surfsup10:	Luv it!
JayKae:	Seriously?
Surfsup10:	Yeah, seriously. Luv old stuff. What's the weather like?
JayKae:	Here? Now?
Surfsup10:	Yeah
JayKae:	About 50, raining a little. What time is it there?
Surfsup10:	9:00 P.M. What time there?
JayKae:	1:00 A.M.
Surfsup10:	Do u have school?
JayKae:	Yeah. Just sometimes I can't sleep. Can I email u?
Surfsup10:	If u tell me ur real name and something about ur self.
JayKae:	Jason Kovak. I'm a junior at Ingraham High School.
Surfsup10:	k
JayKae:	k But what's ur name?
Surfsup10:	Allison Gray
JayKae:	That's pretty. I'll email you tomorrow
Surfsup10:	k Sweet dreams, Jason.

And I did. I had very sweet dreams. So sweet that I stopped thinking about Dad's shocking news. In fact, as I went to bed that night, I decided the first thing I would do in the morning was

E-mail Allison Gray. Her last words were playing in my mind like a three-word song, over and over. Sweet dreams, Jason . . . sweet dreams, Jason . . . what a sweet dream she was! Bomb. Undoubtedly bomb. I could just see Allison Gray surfing across the waves on a Maui beach. A golden girl, wet and shimmering in the sparkling sun. Luscious.

But my dreams of Allison Gray were so sweet that I overslept. This really pissed me off because I didn't have time to send an E-mail. But I was thinking of her from the moment I opened my eyes. *Allison Gray*, I thought as I looked at the clock. *Allison Gray*, I even said her name as I rushed in the shower and said it again as I jumped in my clothes. *Allison Gray*. I grabbed a bagel. *Allison Gray*. I got my coat. *Allison Gray*. I locked the front door and left the house, thinking I could hardly wait for this day to be over so I could be back in the privacy of my own home sending her an E-mail.

But as I ran to the bus stop a thought pierced my brain like the steel blade of a surgeon's knife. *What if Allison Gray was a guy?*

Oh my God. You always heard about that stuff on the Net. How would I ever know? Not that I have any problem with gay people. Kenny's neighbors, Greg and Ron, are great guys. And I remember what Bertha Jane said, too. "There's so little love in this world, Jason, we must honor it wherever we find it." Bertha Jane was like that, she thought love was a bigger deal than sex. Which is fine, but I'd like to have some of both, with a girl.

On the bus I sat in the back and put on my Discman. The bus was pretty quiet this morning; some people were asleep and a few were playing cards. And as usual there was the camera, that big eye bolted to the front of the bus, recording every move anyone made. It's supposed to record fights and crime, but it usually just tapes people bouncing along on the bus attending to their bodies—combing their hair, scratching, poking pimples, putting on make-up, picking their noses—activities like that. There sure isn't much privacy in this world—security cameras, locker searches for weapons and drugs. At least no one has figured out a way to read minds yet, because if they read mine, it would not be for a general audience.

I was back in Maui with Allison Gray. Right then and there I decided that there was enough stress in my life without adding the fear that Allison Gray was a guy. What the hell, we'd never meet anyway, so I might as well have a good time and enjoy dreaming of her.

I took my earphones off while I changed CDs. Since Allison Gray said she liked old stuff, I decided to listen to some. I leafed through my soft case looking for the Grateful Dead. While I looked, my earphones were off, and I overheard the two girls in front of me.

"Last night he told me to take out the garbage and all I said was, 'Why do I have to now, why can't I do it in the morning?' And my stepdad says, 'Because I said so.' I hate that, I really do."

"Mine says the same thing!"

I put my earphones back on and listened to the Dead. And I started to wonder what Doreen Kemple would be like as a step-mother and also what kind of guy my stepbrother was. Doreen Kemple was blond, maybe her kid was blond, too. And she was on the plump side. Not fat, just pudgy. She and my dad had that in common, they were both round. They also had the Beasley Motivation Seminar in common, which is where they met. I pictured this seventeen-year-old male who looked like Miss Piggy and realized that my new stepbrother could be a dork.

On my way to my first-period class, I saw Kenny and Kimberly holding hands, and she was smiling at him like they shared a secret. Their getting back together came as no surprise to me, but I am still hella depressed by this.

"Hey, Kovak, wassup?" Kenny pulled her closer, dropped her hand, and put his arm around her.

"Hi, Jason." Kimberly leaned into him, almost putting her head on his shoulder.

"Not much." I looked up at the clock. "Gotta get to class."

"Great game last night, huh?" Kenny called over his shoulder as they continued down the hall.

"Yeah, thanks," I mumbled, knowing there wouldn't be a next game unless they had another fight.

In my first-period class, which is Language Arts, we're supposed to write in our journals. As I pulled mine out of my backpack, it occurred to me that when my stepbrother arrives, I might get stuck with him. I could lose all my free time and privacy because this dork would be stickin' to me like a tick on a dog.

I got more and more bummed about this, and since I was in class where I couldn't do the things that usually help my mood (listen to music or mess around on the Net), I decided to write Thao. I started a letter to her in the middle of my journal.

Dear Thao,

How is everything in California? I hope it is better than when I talked to you last week. I am sorry I have not been able to call again. Dad is starting to say things about the money I spend and I know he wants me to get a job. I guess I just don't want to work for anyone but Bertha Jane. But I know I will have to start looking soon.

Last night Dad told me that he is going to get married again. This really surprised me since I thought he was enjoying being single. The woman he is going to marry has a son and they are all going to come to live with us.

Thao, please don't think I'm a jerk, but I am not really happy about this news. Not that I don't want my dad to be happy, if this is what he wants. But I feel a lot like the way I did when my mother got married to Henry Lott after she dumped Bob Scanlon. Do you remember my talking about him? Bob Scanlon was the guy she lived with on the houseboat when she first moved out. He had a BMW with his initials on it and I

rammed his fender one time. Well, her relationship with him did not work out and she
was single for a while. But when I heard she
was going to marry Henry Lott it bothered
me because I knew then that my parents
would not get back together. I know this all
sounds so crazy to you, since divorce is not
so common in Vietnam. Actually, it sounds
crazy to me. But I had to tell someone
about it. Please write soon, Thao.
     Love,
     Jason

I closed my notebook just as the bell rang. I felt a little less down after writing Thao. Part of my job at Bertha Jane's had been to help her with English, but as I mentioned, our conversations probably helped me as much or more than they helped Thao. Before I worked there, I had been terrified of girls and this is not an exaggeration. I was extremely interested in them, but talking to girls took as much nerve as it would for me to bungee-jump. (I am someone who is afraid of heights.) And it wasn't just girls. I actually couldn't talk to anyone very easily. "Shy" is too lame a word to describe my problem, but Thao changed everything. Thao and Bertha Jane. Looking back on it, I realize now that when Bertha Jane made it part of my job to help Thao, it helped my confidence. It put me in the position of offering someone something they needed. In the past I've been quite an expert at avoidance, but because it was a job and I had to go there every day, it kept me from panicking and fleeing the whole situation. In a nutshell, I guess you'd say I was forced to help someone and it helped me.

Thao was sweet and beautiful and I felt important to her when we'd work on her class assignments. I even got up the nerve to ask her out. Naturally, I felt pretty destroyed when she turned me down. But Bertha Jane got me to understand that in Vietnam, girls Thao's age didn't date and even though her parents weren't here, she didn't want to do anything that would upset them.

In some ways, knowing all we could be was friends took some pressure off. It's easy to tell her what's on my mind since I don't have to try to be cool. All I have to do is write things clearly and use the right words because she is learning English, but other than that I don't have to worry about what I say. I'm really freed up with Thao.

It's funny, but when I wrote her about Bob Scanlon, I realized I hadn't thought about him in a long time. Him and his stupid BMW. I hated that car. It was one time after I had one of my ridiculous visits with him and Mom on their houseboat (the kind where the TV's on and no one talks), that I had a little go at his car in the parking lot. I was getting in my beater when I noticed his perfect, gleaming, new, blue BMW with its vanity license plate SCANLON. When I started my car I began to hum amusement park–type organ music and it was as if I was in one of those little bumper cars zipping around bumping into all the other little cars and ZIP! I just backed right into Scanlon's car. I did it several times while humming. I never told anyone this until I wrote to Thao today in Language Arts.

As I left class, I kept thinking about how my family was going to change *again*. I cringed thinking about my stepbrother, this dorky guy with a Miss Piggy face, riding the bus with me, following me down the hall, eating lunch with me, scarfing down something disgusting, greasy food stuck to his pudgy face. He better sleep in the bedroom upstairs, 'cause I don't want the dork anywhere near my stuff.

It was all very depressing. Sometimes when I get depressed all I want to do is sleep; that's how it was right after Bertha Jane died. I didn't want to do anything. I didn't even turn on my computer because I didn't care about anything, only sleep. I would come home from school and go to bed. A few hours later I'd wake up and eat something, then I'd watch TV until late, sometimes an old movie until one or two in the morning, or a video.

But today when I got home, for the first time since Bertha Jane died and Thao left, I didn't sleep. Even though I was depressed about my dork stepbrother, I also had Allison Gray to think about. All day I had been a yo-yo going back and forth, first feeling bummed about the dork, and then getting psyched about E-mailing Allison Gray. It had been a weird day, back and forth so much that I was starting to feel slightly nuts.

I grabbed a banana in the kitchen and then went down to my room and turned on the computer. While I waited for AOL to come on, I peeled the banana and ate some, then when AOL came on and the guy said, "You have mail," I was so excited to get the E-mail from Allison Gray that I gagged.

Acckkk! My tongue is hanging out of my mouth and I'm gagging and gagging on the banana. "*Acckkk! Ackkk!*" I keep gagging as I see the E-mail come on the screen. I run to the bathroom and gulp down some water, trying to get a little control before I read Allison's E-mail.

When I got back to the computer there were two E-mails on the screen.

> YouCanBeAspy@aol.com   Be A SPY on the Internet!
> Hawepi66@aol.com   Personal Assistant/Exercise Trainer Needed in SoCal

There is nothing from Surfsup10. I picked up the half-eaten banana, which I had left next to my computer, and took a bite. Chewing slowly, I opened the E-mail, although I knew it would be junk. Total crap. It always happens after you've been in a chat room. AOL won't give out its membership lists, so people who want to sell stuff get in the chat rooms and rip off the E-mail addresses and start sending stuff as fast as they can. It's the American way. I opened the first one, which said:

> Learn everything about your friends, neighbors, enemies, employees or anyone else!—even your boss—even yourself! My mammoth "ONLINE

DETECTIVE KIT" of Internet sites will provide you over FIVE HUNDRED giant resources to look up people, credit, social security, current or past employment, mail order purchases, addresses, phone numbers, maps to city locations. Locate an old friend (or enemy who is hiding) or a lost love—Find E-mail, telephone or address information on anyone! Even look up "unlisted" phone numbers! My huge collection is ONLY THE BEGINNING! Once you locate these FREE private, college, and government web sites, you'll find even MORE links to even MORE information search engines! Send $19.75 cash, check or money order to:

PC Investigations
P.O. Box 21285
Columbus, OH 43221-0185

Detective kit, yeah sure. Some diphead was trying to get money for government Web sites. I hit "delete," then opened the next one.

Affluent La Jolla, CA Marketing Exec. Seeks Full Time Exercise Trainer/
General Assistant Call Toll Free 1-888-366-6709
Greetings . . .
    Hopefully you'll find the headline above and the sincere search that it prefaces to be of interest to you or to someone you know, and won't consider this to be anything other than it is, an honest attempt to match up an open opportunity with an individual who's right for it. An immediate (yes, someone could start tomorrow!) opening exists that's begging to be filled in beautiful sunny and warm Southern California (San Diego area with possible imminent relocation north to the Malibu area) by just the right person. What might that person be like? Well, first of all, this lucrative opportunity (it's really not like most other traditional jobs) loaded with generous bonuses, travel and an enjoyable lifestyle can only be filled by a single (not currently in an encumbered romantic relationship) female who has no children to care for. Ultimate freedom and flexibility is a must. She's a warm, attractive (preferably petite and very feminine), personable, vivacious, upbeat and adventurous woman who has an affinity for working out, staying very fit and being

on the cutting edge of healthy living. She can tailor and coach an exercise program (stretching, weight training, cardio and sports massage) for a man who's committed to excellence in all areas of his life. So what's he like? He's an accomplished, youthful, early 40's direct marketer with a history of successes to his credit. He's warm, generous, sometimes funny, considered brilliant and is a devoted lifetime learner. He loves film and music, is a good traveler, enjoys rollerblading, scuba diving, getting an allover tan and experiencing and sharing as much of life as he can. Compensation is negotiable, upscale room and board being provided to the right candidate would be a preferred provision of an overall package. Call 1-888-366-6709. Thanks for reading and have a great time on line!

After I read this I picked up the phone and called that number. A guy answers with a recorded message: "Greetings. Thanks for calling, please leave your name, number, time zone, and E-mail address. I'll do my best to return your call as soon as I can. Do whatever it takes to make it a great day and take care of yourself."

Beep.

"Get a life, diphead!" I yell in the phone, then I hang up.

I don't know why this guy got me so mad. But if I ever met him I'd want to punch his face. Even the fake detective kit was better than this scum. I could just see someone like Thao down there in California, who is so sweet and doesn't know what's going on, getting taken in by scum like this. "Upscale room and board would be a preferred provision." What a lot of crap. He wants someone to live in his upscale room, do whatever he wants for no money. Sounds like slavery to me. I start to call him up again and tell him what a pervert he is, but as I'm reaching for the phone I stop myself. An argument starts in my head.

"You're the one who should get a life! What's wrong with you? Sitting here calling perverts from the Net so you can scream at someone!"

"So? Got any better ideas? Besides the pervert deserves it."

"Yeah, here's a better idea. E-mail Allison Gray."

"She's probably a fake, too. Just like that scum who wants a slave."

"So if she is fake, you can handle it. Remember what Bertha Jane said. There are so many disappointments in life we might as well celebrate whatever possibilities come along."

When Bertha Jane came into my head like that, I had to smile. I remembered how she ran for mayor even though she had no chance of winning. Maybe that was what was wrong with me—I never took chances.

I clicked on "Compose Mail" and put Allison's E-mail address in the address box. Then I sat there staring at the blank box. I sat there so long that I got a message saying "Please Wake Up. You are still on-line." That seemed to get me in gear and I started writing. In the place where it said subject I wrote "Chat."

I looked at it and deleted it. *Dumb.*

Then I wrote "Hi." Then I deleted that. *Boring.*

Finally I wrote "Wassup." Then I looked at the message box and stared some more. Trying to write an E-mail to Allison Gray was worse than homework, worse than writing a story for Language Arts when I couldn't think of anything to write. I looked at my watch, trying to figure out what time it was in Hawaii. I think they are four hours later than we are, so it must be around eight there. Maybe she was already on-line and we could send instant messages. I finally decided just to say that.

> Hi Allison,
> Remember me? Jason Kovak from Seattle. R u on-line now? I'll stay
> on for a while and if you get this, how 'bout sending me an instant
> message? Do whatever it takes to have a great day and take care of
> yourself!
> Jason

While I was waiting for Allison to possibly send me an instant message, I decided to go in a chat room. I've noticed that the chat rooms are usually full of West Coast kids from four to six when the rents aren't home from work. A few weeks ago I was home with the flu and got on-line and I noticed that when it was one here, it was four back East and the rooms were full of East Coast kids. Then it hit me. *I got the time screwed up.* It wasn't eight in Hawaii, it was noon! Allison would still be in school. Hella lousy. I sat in front of the screen looking at the chat.

APlusLETTR:	yeah
HFPTFS:	Anyone from NJ?
Clkorj:	this is a boring room?
Gigglerboy:	19 m wants 16 fem to talk to
HFPTFS:	in ur dreams
Ston102516:	NO ONE #@#X WITH N E ONE WHILE STON IS HERE
APlusLETTR:	oh scarin' me
Ston102516:	HAHA
Clkorj:	oh Ok ston! Now we're all scared!

I was sitting there reading all this garbage when the little instant message screen popped down.

Surfsup10:	Hi Jason, Wassup? We got outta school early, so I checked out my mail. Great to hear from you? R u on-line now? Let me know. Later— Allison

My hands were sweating as I answered.

JayKae:	Hey, wassup? I'm here, just hanging in a chat room?
Surfsup10:	N E good chat?
JayKae:	No, just the usual crap.
Surfsup10:	it's so stupid.
JayKae:	i know.

Surfsup10:	So, tell me about urself Jason?
JayKae:	Not a lot to tell.
Surfsup10:	Oh, i'm sure there is. r u a shy guy?
JayKae:	I guess you cud say that.
Surfsup10:	Wat du u like in a female?
JayKae:	Someone warm, attractive, personable, upbeat, adventurous
Surfsup10:	That's me! More about u!
JayKae:	U really wanna know?
Surfsup10:	OF COURSE!
JayKae:	I'm warm, generous, sometimes funny, considered brilliant.
Surfsup10:	Mmmm U sound very mature.
JayKae:	People tell me that.
Surfsup10:	Wat d u like 2 do?
JayKae:	Rollerblading, scuba diving.
Surfsup10:	Scuba diving? Thought you were from Seattle?
JayKae:	I am. I know it sounds crazy. But we dive here, gotta wear a wet suit.
Surfsup10:	Cool. so what else is new, Jason?
JayKae:	I'm gonna have this dork for a stepbrother.
Surfsup10:	That sux.
JayKae:	I know.
Surfsup10:	A real creep, huh?
JayKae:	I'm gonna b stuck with him.
Surfsup10:	Just drop him off at a mall and say you'll pick him up and then go party.
JayKae:	I'll try that.
Surfsup10:	Send a pic, Jason. k?
JayKae:	Don't have a new 1. I've changed a lot since last year.
Surfsup10:	Get a new 1, k?
JayKae:	k. u 2?
Surfsup10:	k i gotta get off. Later, Jason. Luv chattin with ya!

JayKae:	Me 2. How 'bout tomorrow? Time?
Surfsup10:	'Bout 12.
JayKae:	Midnight?
Surfsup10:	Noon. We get out early all week cuz of teachers meetings.
JayKae:	k. 4, my time. Later, Allison. Peace

I turned off my computer and went up to the kitchen and got a Coke. I felt quite happy and also a little nuts. Why did I tell her that stuff from the pervert's E-mail? About scuba diving and rollerblading, two things I've never done in my life. I can't tell you how many times I do stuff and I don't even know why. I am thinking about this and then the voices get going again.

"It's no big thing, telling her that stuff from the pervert's E-mail. What're you going to do, tell her the truth? That all you do is talk to your dog, feed birds, and pick your nose?"

"What if I meet her someday?"

"Visit reality. You're never going to meet her. Hawaii's hardly Tacoma."

"You're right. I'll never meet her."

But someone I *was* going to meet pretty soon was Josh Kemple, Mr. Piggy, my dork stepbrother. As I sipped on my Coke, I began to wonder what it might be like for him. It was like Bertha Jane had gotten in my brain again and was trying to tell me something. "Kindness is its own reward, Jason." I could almost hear her voice, the memory of her words was so powerful. I knew Bertha Jane wouldn't want me to be mean to Josh Kemple. She would probably tell me that he probably didn't want this situation any more than I did. In fact, it had to be worse for him. Having to move in his senior year, graduating with a class where he didn't know a single person. He probably would be a really lonely guy.

I knelt down and patted Fred. I guess I could let Fred sleep in his room some nights, maybe. And I wouldn't drop him off at a mall and then go somewhere without him. Even though he was a dork, I'd hang with him some, I decided. Then I smiled. Bertha Jane would approve. I remember her saying, "We can't save humanity, Jason, but we can live in this world in small, useful ways that touch other human beings."

Actually, one human being I would like to touch is Allison Gray. I would like to get it on with her, and not just on-line.

📁 Three

THE NEXT DAY AFTER the last bell, Kenny came up to me at my locker and I was shocked when I saw him. He looked like he spent the night in a garbage can. I'd never seen him looking so terrible. He was just a mess, like a raccoon or a fighter with big dark rings under his eyes where someone had punched his lights out. Some guys stagger into school like that after they've gotten totally wasted the night before, but Kenny didn't mess around with that kind of stuff and it really worried me just to look at him.

"Hey, Jason." Kenny's voice was so quiet, I could hardly hear him.

"What happened to you, man?"

"We broke up."

"You and Kimberly?" Dumb question. Who else would it be?

"Yeah."

"Sorry to hear that." Here we go again, is what I thought, but I didn't want to say it, he looked so awful.

"What are you doing?"

"Now? Just getting my stuff together so I can catch the bus."

"How 'bout if I stop over?"

"Sure. But could you make it a little later? I told my dad I'd pick up some stuff for him before dinner." A little lie, of course. But I could hardly tell him I didn't want him hanging with me at four when I had my cyberdate. That was how I had been thinking about it all day, my cyberdate. Not as good as the real thing in flesh and blood and living color, but still—a date. A date to connect with a girl. (Unless it was a guy. Occasionally, I still had those nagging little doubts.)

It was raining as I went to the bus. I found a seat next to the window and as I looked out at the parking lot, I saw Kenny walking slowly, and not moving the way people usually do in the rain, fast, with their heads down. His head was straight and the rain hit his face as if he didn't care what happened to him.

The bus left school and as we stopped at the light across from the lot, I watched Kenny get in his car, but he didn't put the key in the ignition. Instead, he put his head down on the steering wheel. Then the light changed and the bus pulled away. I felt bad that I hadn't told him he could come right over, and of course, an argument started in my head.

"Some friend."

"Yeah, when he has a girlfriend he's never there for me."

"Like you have a girlfriend? Ha! Cyberdate? Pathetic."

"He's coming over at five. It's not like I won't see him soon."

That's what I told myself so I wouldn't worry about him, but I worried anyway. He seemed more upset than how he gets after his usual fights with Kimberly. Maybe cyber-relationships were the best kind to have after all, so you wouldn't get clobbered and be messed up like Kenny was today. If a cyber-relationship ended, you'd just miss words coming into your computer. It wouldn't be like not hearing a girl's voice or looking in her eyes, or touching her.

But by four I wasn't thinking about Kenny anymore. I was right there in front of my trusty PC, glued to it, poised for action. I clicked on AOL, typed in my password, which is SPIDER. I chose it because spiders have been very important in my life. Ever since my mom taught me "The Itsy Bitsy Spider" I have been fond of them. I know this sounds strange. But I never kill them, I scoop them up and put them outside. My password could actually be FRIEND OF SPIDERS, but that would make it too long. In the song the spider was trying to get up the water spout and it got washed away, but when the sun came out it just tried again. I like that.

And right now I am trying again to get a female in my life. After I typed in SPIDER, I waited while AOL came on and then I heard music. Not real music, but certainly music to my ears. It was the AOL computer voice and the guy said the magic words, the words I had been waiting for: "You've Got Mail!"

"YES!" I yelled so loud, I guess I scared Fred because he barked. I patted his head while I clicked on the yellow envelope and the E-mail came on. There it was . . . Surfsup10!

To: JayKae
From: Surfsup10
Subject: Life stinx
Hi Jason,
i am so pissed. i'm grounded! The whole thing really sux too. i got caught skipping and the school called my mom. We only had a half day cuz of their stupid teacher meetings and i thought with the schedule being changed i wouldn't get caught. But i did and now i can't do n e thing! i begged her to let me send a couple of emails so my friends wouldn't think i'm dead. She said ok, but this is the last u will hear from me for a while. i can't get on the Net, talk on the phone, or go out or n e thing for 2 weeks. The whole thing is so stupid. it's not like we got drunk or shoplifted. My mother is being totally bizarre about this. So i just wanted u to know. i'll E-mail u in 2 weeks.
Later,
Allison

I read her message over a couple of times, feeling worse each time. Just my luck! Just when I finally found something to look forward to for the first time since Thao left and Bertha Jane died, and it's gone. Poof! Down the toilet.

I wondered why she'd skipped class. Maybe to go surfing. I began to picture her in my mind, this bomb girl with her bomb friends prancing out of the school with their little bathing suits on under their clothes. They would roar off to the beach in their bright red convertible with its top down, their hair blowing in the warm, tropical breeze. At the beach, they'd hop out of the car and leap across the beach, giggling like girls do, and then they'd take off their clothes and go frolicking in the waves. It must be very hard to stay in school when you live in a place like Hawaii.

Damn. Two weeks is a long time. I didn't want Allison Gray to forget me, so I decided I better stop daydreaming about her and write a reply. Then when the two weeks were up, there I'd be, right in her computer waiting for her, like a faithful, steady, spot-on guy.

To: Surfsup10
From: JayKae
Subject: Two weeks
Hi Allison,
Bummer, being grounded for 2 weeks. I'll miss chatting with u. Well,
I'm off to get in a little rollerblading before it gets dark. Don't forget to
email me when you're back on the net.
peace
Jason

I read over the E-mail before I clicked "send." Right. Rollerblading, once again I borrowed stuff from that pervert's life. I looked out the window. Now it was raining even harder, pouring. Oh well. Since I don't have anything to tell about my own boring life, who cares? She'll never find out. And at least it gives me something to say. No way could I tell her the pathetic truth, that she's all I've been thinking about since the day I first found her in the chat room.

Then I heard the doorbell upstairs, so I hit "send," shut off my computer, and ran up to get it. Kenny stood at the door with his collar pulled up and his hands jammed in his pockets, looking like a totally wasted person.

He mumbled "hi" and came in, moving like he was in a trance. "Pretty bummed, huh?" I went to the refrigerator, got us each a Coke.

"Yeah." Kenny slumped at the kitchen table and stared out at the rain.

"What happened? I mean, you've had fights before?"

"This is different."

"Oh."

We didn't say anything. Just looked out at the rain and sipped our Cokes.

"Want anything to eat?"

"Not hungry." Kenny took a swig of his Coke.

Silence. I didn't know what to say to cheer him up. Besides, usually I don't have to worry about talking with Kenny, he's always been the one who talks.

"You always get back together," I finally said.

"Not this time. She dumped me."

"Did she think you had something going with Rhondelle Jackson again?"

"No. She dumped me for another guy."

"For another guy? Seriously?"

"You got it." Kenny looked away like he didn't want me to see his face.

"Who?"

"No one we know. He's a senior at Franklin."

"So how does she know this guy?"

"They both sing in that all-city chorus. I guess she's been with him every Saturday for months. The guy just kept moving in on her."

"Jeez."

"I'd like to stuff my fist down his throat so he'd never sing again."

"Just rip the hell out of his vocal cords."

"Yeah. And bash his face in while I'm at it."

Then Kenny started going on about all the evil stuff he was going to do to the guy and it was beginning to sound like a combo of *Friday the Thirteenth* and *The Texas Chainsaw Massacre*. It got gross, but it seemed to make him feel better. He even wanted to cruise a little, so we got in his car and drove to the U district and cruised up and down the Ave. After awhile he got hungry, so we stopped at Burger King. Kenny wasn't really into it though, I could tell by the ketchup. He usually asks for extra and squishes about four of those little foil packages, drowning his burger. I think it's kind of a mess, actually, but that's the way he likes it. But today his burger was more like a normal person's. Weird for him though, since he just used one of those little packages. But at least he had wanted to eat something and I thought that was a good sign. After we had eaten, we couldn't think of anything else to do and just decided to go home.

But on the way to drop me off, he took a right turn on McClellan instead of a left to my street.

"Kenny?"

"Yeah."

"You go left on McClellan to get to my house."

"I know that."

I could tell by the way he stared straight ahead that he didn't want to talk. For a second it even occurred to me that he might want to do something crazy like drive right into the lake or something. But I really didn't think Kenny was the type. And if he did want to kill himself, he wouldn't do it with me in the car. Besides I would never let him do that. I don't know how I would stop him, but I would. I wouldn't be someone whose friend killed himself and the person said he had no clue. I know Kenny's messed up, and I just would never let him do anything stupid like that.

Then I saw where he was headed: Kimberly's house. He drove down her street and parked out front. We just sat there and all Kenny did was just stare at her house.

"Listen, man, girls are nutso about you. You'll get another one. And better than her, too."

"I just want *her*."

Then he jammed the car in gear and my head snapped as he peeled off. He looked miserable all over again, and I was trying to think of what I could say to help.

What would Bertha Jane say? And I smiled a little inside, with the feeling I get when I remember Bertha Jane and something she said. Bertha Jane always quoted some comedian, I forgot which one, but the guy said, "Ninety percent of life is showing up." I remember when I didn't quite get it and Bertha Jane explained it to me. "Well, Jason, if you think about it, it means showing up for work, showing up for school, showing up at home, showing up when a friend is sick, things like that. That's about it. That's about all you have to do." And I knew I had showed up for Kenny. Even though I stopped at my house first to check my E-mail, I had still showed up.

It wasn't raining as hard as we headed toward my street, but it was dark now. The wet pavement glistened and the streetlight shone in a big puddle in front of my house where the sewer was clogged.

"Looks like you've got a lake here."

"Yeah." I opened the door and as I climbed out, Kenny put his hand on my arm.

"Thanks."

I put my arm around his shoulder for a minute, then I felt dumb so I took it away and got out of the car. But I left the door open and leaned in.

"It's going to be okay, man. You'll see."

Kenny just nodded and looked away, so I shut the door and went in the house.

• • •

I was in the den watching the Sonics when I heard a car drive up. I didn't hear the sound of the garage door, so I didn't think it was Dad. Maybe Kenny forgot something or just wanted to hang some more. But the next thing I heard was the back door opening, then a big slam. Then I heard Dad yelling as he came roaring in the house.

"Where the hell were you, Jason!" He stood in the doorway of the den having a complete meltdown. "I've been out driving around trying to find you!"

"What're you talking about?" I stared at him, clueless.

"It's Thursday night," he roared. "We're having dinner at Doreen's so we can meet Josh."

"Oh. Guess I forgot."

"We just told you two nights ago. How could you forget?"

"I just did."

"Well, come on! Let's go!"

"Now?"

He went to the TV and snapped if off. "Of course, now! We're already a half hour late. Go change your shirt while I call her and tell her we're on our way."

"What's wrong with my shirt?"

"It's got your lunch on the front!"

Dad usually doesn't notice what I have on; in fact, this is one kind of hassle I haven't had to put up with since Mom left. But he was furious, so I went to change.

Most of my clothes are all over the place in my room, and I wasn't sure if I had anything that was clean. I looked in my closet and there were a couple of shirts hanging up, stuff I never wear. One was a shirt Mom sent me for Christmas. A light blue dress shirt, nothing I'd wear to school. But it was clean, never been worn, in fact, so I grabbed it.

Dad didn't say a word as we drove to Doreen's. I wasn't exactly sure where we were going, all I knew was that she lived in some waterfront condo on Lake Washington. As we drove along the boulevard, I looked across the lake at the floating bridge that went to Mercer Island. Watching the headlights moving along in a steady stream, you could almost get hypnotized, which I don't think I'd mind too much. It might be kind of fun. You could walk and talk but you'd actually be nicely asleep and would have no memory of anything that happened.

I used to drive over the Montlake Bridge to get to Mom's houseboat when she first moved out. That's where she lived with Bob Scanlon. At first I didn't think I knew how Kenny felt getting dumped by Kimberly Cotton. But when I remembered driving across the Montlake Bridge going to see Mom, I realized I did know. Not that a mother is a girlfriend or anything weird like that, but she dumped us. She left me and Dad and went to be with that diphead. I hated that guy, with his beamer and his stupid shirts with little alligators on them. I'm glad I bumped into his beamer on purpose. I wish I'd totaled it.

So here we are, with me still not completely used to having Mom gone, about to have this new family. A stepmother and a stepbrother for God's sake. Things were going too fast. I think I would like everything to be going slowly. *Very slowly, breathing deeply, now slowly now, slo-o-o-o-w-le-e-ey, your eyes are getting heavy. Tick-tock . . . tick-tock . . . tick-tock . . . follow the watch as it moves back and forth . . . back and forth . . . back and forth . . . Heavy now . . . heavy . . . heavier . . . you are now asleep. Deeply asleep.*

As Dad parked the car and we walked across the lot to Doreen's condo, I was still very awake (hypnotizing myself didn't work), and all I could think about was my dork stepbrother and how I was really going to need all the help I could get from Bertha Jane to be nice to this guy. I've got to remember that life would be hard for a guy who spent his whole life moving from place to place. He was probably so bummed about this that he ate and ate. He was probably more than chubby like his mother. He was probably huge. And when you eat and eat like that, mostly potato chips and candy bars, you get a lot of zits. I've got to remember about his hard life when I see what a mess he is.

Dad rang the bell and the door immediately flew open. Doreen must have been standing right there.

"Hi! Come in! Come in!" She hugged Dad, then she grabbed me and I almost choked on her perfume. My nose was squashed on her head as she hugged me right near where she must squirt all the perfume. I started to choke and she let me go, then Dad poked me.

"Jason?" he hissed through clenched teeth.

"Oh, yeah. Sorry about being late."

"No problem, I just left everything in the oven on warm," she chirped. Then she grabbed my hand. "Come along, Josh is right here in the living room.

I took a deep breath, trying to focus on being a kind and understanding person as she pulled me into the living room.

A guy was standing in the middle of the room, sticking his hand out to shake mine.

"Hi, I'm Josh."

I don't remember what I said or if I shook his hand (although I must have). All I remember is standing in the middle of Doreen Kemple's living room with the top of my head even with her son's armpits. Josh Kemple was huge. And not fat huge, but huge like a giant tree. Like a guy who benches two hundred pounds as if he were lifting a curtain rod.

I had found it easier to talk to people since Bertha Jane and Thao had been in my life, but the sight of Josh Kemple was like a laser that flash-froze my vocal cords. Not only did he look like one of the vanilla guys in the NBA, but his face (which I had expected to be puffy and zitty from his miserable life) bore a strong resemblance to the movie star in *Titanic*. The one that all girls are loony about. The one they crave, the one who makes them totally mental. I know girls who have been renting that video every weekend for years, and *that* is exactly who my stepbrother-to-be Josh Kemple looked like.

"Come on, everybody sit down." Doreen motioned for us to come to the table at the end of the L-shaped living room. "Maybe I should have told you all to bring your sunglasses." She laughed, pointing at the tablecloth. Bright was too dull a word for the thing.

It was almost Day-Glo orange, with huge magenta poppies and blue hummingbirds on it. She had green carnations in the middle of the table and the plates were bright red. "I love color," she said.

"We noticed, honey." Dad smiled at her.

Honey.

"It's so gray in Seattle, I think we need to just brighten and cheer everything up." She grinned.

I looked around her condo, noticing it for the first time. The walls were bright pink, and all the furniture was yellow like lemons. There were candy-striped and plaid pillows on the couches and chairs with green, pink, and yellow stripes. Every wall had framed prints of famous paintings, the kind you get at Pay 'n Save. There was something about it that made me think of a clown's house, it was trying so hard to be cheery.

Doreen went to the kitchen to get the food. "Need some help, honey?" Dad called after her.

Honey again? I looked at the green carnations in the middle of the table. They looked like the kind that were dyed. Mom hated those.

"Nope, I've got it," she called from the kitchen. "Josh and Jason, you sit across from each other and Jack and I will sit on the ends."

"I always sit on my end." Dad chuckled, pulling out his chair.

Doreen came in carrying a big dish of lasagna and a basket of garlic bread and threw back her head and laughed, a big guffaw. She kept laughing like Dad was funny enough to do stand-up in a comedy club.

Josh went "Ha." A little courtesy laugh.

I stared at the dyed carnations and the big magenta poppies and blue hummingbirds on the tablecloth and wondered what I was doing there. Beam me up, Scotty.

"I'll get the salad." Josh went in the kitchen.

"Thanks, honey." Doreen smiled at Josh, then sat across from Dad.

Honey, honey. Where's Pooh Bear? And Rabbit.

Doreen dished out the lasagna and passed around the plates.

"Isn't this nice, all these "J" men? You all have the same initials!"

"Good thing we don't have monogrammed shirts!" Dad chuckled, helping himself to the salad and then passing it to Josh.

Doreen threw her head back again and roared.

Another courtesy laugh from Josh as he heaped salad on his plate.

I grabbed the garlic bread and stuffed some in my face.

Dad put his fork down and picked up his wine glass. "We've got some great news and I think we ought to have a little toast."

Now what? Josh raised his Pepsi can, looking at Dad. Doreen raised her glass and Dad looked at me, waiting for me to join in. I felt like I was toast as I held up my Pepsi an inch off the table, wishing I was somewhere else. *I'm just a little black rain cloud hovering over the honey tree.*

"Josh is going to be able to play for the Ingraham Rams!" Dad announced in a big, booming voice. "We've had a waiver from the athletic department. Usually a player has to be enrolled for a semester before they can be on the team the following season. But Doreen and I petitioned for a waiver and Tom Williams, the Ingraham basketball coach, called today to tell me that it's been approved."

"Awesome." Josh grinned and swigged his Pepsi.

I gulped mine.

"We didn't want to say anything until we had definite word," Dad explained, setting down his glass and picking up his fork again. "But even as a junior all the college scouts were looking at Josh and it would have been a real tragedy if he had missed his senior season."

"How's the team?" Josh looked at me.

"Okay, I guess."

"Last year they came in second in the city," Dad chimed in.

"You play any sports?" Josh tore himself a piece of garlic bread.

"Not really."

"What're you into?"

"Oh, I mess with computers." I'm sure I could tell him that I feed birds.

"Cool."

"Josh was the leading scorer on his team ever since his freshman year," Doreen bragged. Then she got on a roll, telling about what a great player he was, how every time they moved and he went to a new school, he ended up being the star of that team. On and on, with Dad eating it up.

"I was going to stay in Chicago and finish the year there, but it didn't work out." Josh looked sad for a minute.

"He has the most beautiful girlfriend." Doreen helped herself to more lasagna. "Show everyone Megan's picture, Josh."

Josh pulled a photo out of his wallet. "Her dad got sick, so I couldn't stay there."

"That's too bad." I meant it. I react differently from how I used to when I hear things like that. Ever since Bertha Jane died, I feel more sad for people. Even for his beautiful girlfriend's father that I didn't even know.

"He got diabetes and he has to change his diet and a bunch of stuff and I guess they thought it wasn't a good time to have another kid living there." Josh handed me a picture from his wallet.

I glanced at the photo and handed it back to him. "Nice." Awesome was more like it. She looked like a model, but I couldn't bring myself to say anything else.

The dinner might as well have been called The Josh Kemple Show. When we had dessert, Doreen brought out scrapbooks of his great sports career, and Dad practically drooled on every page.

But it got even worse. "There was a time during Josh's junior year that he hit a bit of a slump."

"Air balls, that was all I came up with." Josh laughed.

"So I talked to Josh's father. We've always been able to talk, at least when it came to Josh. And he agreed to send Josh to the Beasley Motivation Seminar. They have them all over the country, you know."

I start gagging on the chocolate-cream pie. Little pieces fly out of my mouth onto the tablecloth.

"Jason!" Dad grabs his napkin pointedly, like he's trying to get me to use mine.

I'm still choking, but I cover my mouth with the napkin. It has magenta poppies and blue hummingbirds on it to match the table-cloth. Then I wipe up the little chocolaty spit pieces that had splattered on the tablecloth. *Dab, dab, dab, wipe up those little buggers . . . clean as a whistle . . . good as new!*

"It really helped. Visualize. Concentrate. I'm telling you, that's the key to everything." Josh grins.

Dad thumps him on the back. "You're a kid after my own heart, Josh."

Dab, dab, dab, dab, dabbity doo. . . . I wipe more spit off the tablecloth.

When we get home, Dad goes whistling up the stairs to his room. He is whistling "Sweet Georgia Brown," the theme song of the Harlem Globetrotters. I go down to my room and call Kenny. It rings a long time and when I get his voice mail, I don't feel like leaving a message so I just hang up.

I took off my shirt and then I did something I haven't done since Christmas. I decided to call Mom. I had to get her number from my desk since I hardly ever talk to her and don't know it by heart. When she first moved, we were supposed to talk once a week. It started out like that, but then I'd just get her voice mail, or she'd get ours and the weekly plan fizzled and sputtered and finally evolved into mainly talking on holidays or my birthday.

I dialed and then hummed a little while it rang. Damn. I was humming "Sweet Georgia Brown." I did not want basketball or anything to do with it getting in my brain without my permission. If I go to a Sonics game, fine. *I'm* choosing to be there. But to be humming a song Dad had been singing because he was psyched about Josh felt like my brain was getting poisoned. I tried to get another song going, but "Sweet Georgia Brown" was stuck and it was starting to totally piss me off. It's bad enough to have my own house about to be invaded, but my brain! Then all of a sudden I realized it was really late back there. No wonder the phone was ringing and ringing. It was ten here so it was like two in the morning there. Oh shit. I started to hang up.

"Yes." A very annoyed, sleepy voice.

"Mom?"

"Who is this?"

"It's Jason."

"Jason? Do you know what time it is?"

"Sorry."

"Is something wrong? Are you hurt?" She sounded more awake.

"No."

"Well, what is it?" *Very, very, annoyed.* "It's very late."

"Nothing."

"Jason, if you just want to talk, call me at a decent hour."

"Okay. Bye."

Then we hung up.

I sat on my bed and looked at the shirt she'd sent for Christmas on the floor on a heap of other stuff. After a few minutes I picked it up and put it on Fred. I used to get a kick out of dressing up the dog when I was a little kid, but it had been years since I'd put any clothes on Fred. His legs got tangled in the sleeves and he couldn't move so I took it off him and went to my desk, scrounging around until I found some scissors. Then I held the shirt sleeves against Fred's leg and measured the right amount for the length. *Snip!* Off came the first sleeve. I held it against his leg. Very nice. It hit slightly above his foot, just enough to make a nice cuff, but a good length so he won't step on it. *Snip!* The other one, a perfect match. Then I cut along the bottom. *Snip, snip, snip,* it would just reach to Fred's butt. (It would spoil the whole look if Fred wore this outside someday and crapped on the shirttail.)

"You look great," I told Fred, who didn't seem to mind as I put the shirt on him again. Then I patted the bed for him to come up.

Fred curled up next to me and I snapped off the light.

There was only one way Fred would ever sleep upstairs with Josh Kemple when he moved in. Over my dead body.

📁 Four

ALLISON GRAY AND I were swimming in the warm ocean. I picked her up and threw her into the surf and she squealed with joy. Then I swam to her and took her in my arms. She kissed me and her lips were warm and she tasted of salt and I carried her out through the waves. Her wet body pressed against mine as I walked through the surf with long, sure-footed strides and put her down on our beach blanket as carefully as if she were spun glass. She lay on her back looking up, inviting me. As I lowered myself to the blanket and began to kiss her again, I felt the earth shaking beneath me. The large leaves on the palm trees were vibrating and I heard a dog howl in the distance. *EARTH-QUAKE?* Terrified, I looked toward the sea and the earth was trembling under the feet of a giant lizard crawling out of the ocean toward us. Green scales fell like acid rain and the lizard screamed, "Get out of Honnalee, you diphead!" Then there was a mighty roar and I covered Allison's body to shield her and the next thing I felt was a huge paw digging into my shoulder. I kept my body over Allison's, desperately trying to protect her while I lashed out with one arm, trying to shoo it away. "*Ackkkk!*" I screamed as more green scales fell like acid rain and splashed against my arm.

"Now you've spilled my coffee!"

"Huh?"

"I've been trying to wake you for the past five minutes." Dad loomed over me wiping his pants, glowering. "I gave you a little shake and you started thrashing around like crazy."

"You could've burned me!" I grabbed the sheet and wiped the coffee off my face.

"It wasn't that hot."

I looked at the clock. "I've still got another half hour before I have to get up." I put the pillow over my head.

"Jason, do you think I just come down here for no reason? I have to leave for work in a minute and I want you to drive over to Doreen's and pick up Josh and take him to school."

"What's wrong with her?"

"Nothing's wrong with her."

"Then what's wrong with you?"

"Nothing's wrong with me!"

"Then why don't one of you take him?"

"Doreen and I thought it would be nice for you boys to go together his first day," he said, getting exasperated.

Not as exasperated as I was. I threw the pillow off my head and sat up. First he ruins a perfectly good dream and now he ruins the morning. "So I'm supposed to be his chauffeur?"

"It's his first day! Why can't you just cooperate for a change! What's wrong with you, Jason?"

"I didn't say I wouldn't do it." I ripped off the covers and went in the bathroom and slammed the door.

While I was in the shower all I could think about was how much I wished things were back like they were when Bertha Jane was alive. When I was with her, it didn't bother me so much that Dad doesn't understand anything about me. And I don't mean that I always understand everything about myself either—there are a lot of things

I just can't explain, like why I do stuff sometimes. But he doesn't even try. That's the whole thing. He doesn't even try to understand how I might feel about anything. It's always just him telling me what to do, how to think, how to be. And I'm never good enough for him. Maybe that was the best thing about being with Bertha Jane. I was good enough for her, just the way I was.

I really didn't want to pick up Josh. We have nothing in common. A guy like Josh is clueless about what it's like to be a walking disappointment to your parents. And on the way to pick him up, I also started worrying about how dumb I would look walking around with him—like an NBA guy and a midget. And what if people didn't get that he was my stepbrother and thought he was my real brother.

"Jeez. What happened to you, Kovak?"

"They only have enough food for one kid in your family?"

"Don't you play *any* sport?"

"Can't believe you guys are brothers!"

We're NOT, *diphead!*

I was having these kinds of conversations as I swung into the parking lot of Doreen's condo. Josh was already outside waiting for me, leaning back against the building by the front door. Just a right and ready guy. On time. You betcha. No hitting the snooze for the fortieth time for this dude.

"Thanks for pickin' me up," he said, opening the door. I keep the seat pulled up pretty far and he had to squish up his body when he got in. He sat with his legs pressed against the dashboard and his knees at his nose.

I knew I should ask him if he wanted me to move my seat back, but I really didn't want to. I mean who would want to drive around with their toes hardly reaching the pedals like an old lady. Why should I be the one to change? Why can't he ride around like a pretzel? It would probably be good for his game, increase his flexibility or something.

But as I put the car in gear and drove out of the lot, I had a strong image of Bertha Jane. She didn't say anything, it was only that she'd come into my mind. Her white wispy hair and her nice old wrinkled face.

"Want me to move the seat back?"

"It's okay. I'm used to it." Josh drew his knees up even closer to his nose.

I reached down to the lever on the side of the seat, pulled it up, and pushed the seat back a little. Not all the way, but enough so I could still drive okay.

"Thanks."

"Sure."

Josh motioned to the radio. "What station do you listen to?"

"KUBE. Sometimes KZOK and 107.7 THE END."

"What do they play?"

"KUBE's hip-hop, sometimes pop and top forty, KZOK's classic rock, like sixties and seventies, and THE END is—"

"The end?"

"It's KNDD, the last spot on the dial so they call it The End. They play alternative rock."

"Almost every station in Chicago was good. Didn't matter what you had on." Josh moved his knees closer to his chin. "How much farther to the school?"

"Couple miles."

"Can you walk there from your house?"

"Depends on how early you start. You could walk to LA if you had a couple of months."

Josh didn't say anything and I felt sort of bad for being a wiseass. "It takes about an hour to walk. I usually ride the bus to save gas money."

"Do they have a second bus for people on teams and stuff?"

"I think they used to but the money got cut or something." I stopped at the light across from the school. "This is it."

"Ingraham." Josh read the name by the front entrance. "Who's Ingraham?"

"Beats me. Some old guy. Local hero or something."

"What's the mascot?"

"Rams."

"Haven't had that one before."

I pulled in the parking lot and Josh thanked me for the ride as we got out of the car. I wondered how many mascots he'd had at all the different schools he went to and actually started to feel bad for him. For a second. A split second is more like it, because as we walked toward the school together, a very amazing thing started happening. Girls materialized out of nowhere. Their heads actually turned to look at him, I mean just pivoting right around on their necks. Some of them didn't even pretend to be doing other stuff while they looked, they just stood and gawked! I couldn't believe they were noticing him so fast!

And as we went in the school, girls I had known all through middle school and even as long ago as elementary school, but who didn't have much to say to me in high school, suddenly remembered they knew me.

"Hi, Jason!" A big smile here from Wendy Freed, who had been in my computer class my freshman year, as she passes us going in the front door.

"Wassup, Jason?" Anne Depue from my old elementary school acts like I'm her best buddy as we go down the hall.

"Oh, Jason! Wait up a minute!" It's none other than Kimberly Cotton, running up to me as Josh and I get to the office.

"Wassup, Kimberly?" We stop outside the office door.

"Jason. I've really got to talk to you." She is panting slightly, a little out of breath from running to catch us.

"Okay."

"Hey, who's your friend?" She looks up at Josh as if she just noticed I was with somebody.

"This is Josh Kemple. My dad's getting married to his mom."

"Cool. Where you from?" Kimberly gushes.

"Chicago."

"Listen, Jason, I want you to call me." She whips open her notebook, scribbles on a piece of paper, rips it off, and shoves it at me. "Here's my number." Then she smiles at Josh and goes bouncing down the hall.

We go in the office and Mr. Williams, the basketball coach, is waiting for us. "Welcome to Ingraham, Josh." They shake hands and Mr. Williams whaps him on the back. "We're sure glad we got that waiver."

Mr. Williams is tall. Not as tall as Josh, but tall enough so that I feel like I am the Sonics ball boy. "I'll take you around to your classes today." He holds out Josh's schedule and points to it. "This is third period here, you've got study hall in room 303. I'll meet you and we can go to my office in the gym. I want to go over the playbook with you before practice this afternoon."

"I can start looking it over now if you want. I'll probably have a few minutes between classes."

Mr. Williams whaps him on the back again. "I like your attitude already!"

"Guess I'll get to class," I mumble.

Mr. Williams looks at me for the first time. He squints his eyes like he's trying to think of something.

"Jason's going to be my stepbrother," Josh explains.

"Who?" Mr. Williams has a blank look.

"Jason, that's me. Jason Kovak."

"Kovak." Mr. Williams repeats my name, but he still has a blank look.

"I'm in your fifth-period PE class."

"Kovak. Right." Mr. Williams nods. But I know and he knows and Josh knows that he doesn't know me from the foot fungus in the locker room. "Hang around your stepbrother here, Jake, maybe some of that talent will rub off." He whaps me on the shoulder.

"You want a ride home after practice?" I ask Josh.

"Don't worry about it, Jake. I'll see that he gets home."

I turn and leave the office. *My name's Jason, you diphead.*

•　•　•

Most of the day I thought about the reception I'd gotten from girls when I arrived at school with Josh. It reminded me of a discussion Kenny and I had one time about how to meet girls. His older brother told him that the best way to meet girls was to get a dog, especially a puppy. All you had to do was walk around with the puppy and you could get any girl you wanted to talk to you. You didn't have to do anything. They'd come right up to you and start the conversation and pat the dog and it wasn't too hard after that to get their phone number. Walking around with Josh is as good as a dog for getting girls to talk to you, but the basic difference is that with a dog the girls can only talk to you, but since Josh is not a dog the girls will talk to him, and I end up feeling as invisible as I did before.

Driving home from school, I also wondered what Kimberly Cotton wanted. It was probably about Kenny and maybe she wanted to talk with me about how he is doing and whether he'd ever want to get back with her. The more I thought about it, the more I decided that was it. It had to be. And even though I have to admit that I liked having a cute girl give me her number in front of Josh, I didn't really want to get in the middle of her thing with Kenny. It would be too easy to say something wrong and end up with both of them mad at me.

As I pulled in the driveway, I saw an orange U-Haul truck parked in front of our house. Then Dad and Tony Brown, a guy who works for him, came out the front door. Tony is younger than my dad, maybe about thirty. He has some tattoos on his arms and is definitely in shape since his job is carrying around portable toilets. Tony and my dad each had an end of our living-room couch. Dad was puffing and grunting.

"Hey *grunt, grunt* Jason! Get over here *grunt, grunt* and give us a hand!" Dad sets his end of the couch down on the front walk. "Come on! Get over here!"

Tony put his end down, too, although he wasn't out of breath. He looked more like he'd been playing a video game than moving furniture.

"I gotta make a call."

"This won't take long. Come on!" Dad wiped the sweat off his face with his shirttail. "Whew! This sucker's heavy."

"How come you're moving the couch? Getting it cleaned or something?"

"We decided to keep Doreen's furniture and sell ours."

"You're selling all our furniture!"

"Not all of it, just the stuff in the living room."

"What's wrong with our stuff!"

"Jason, I don't want to discuss interior decorating. Just pick up the end of the damn couch."

Then Doreen comes out waving strips of paper with colors on them. "Hi, Jason, how was school?"

"Fine," I snarl, grinding my teeth.

"Jack, when you're through there could you come in and help me decide about the living room?"

"Sure, honey." Dad laughs. "If I don't collapse."

Doreen comes over to us and holds out the paint samples. "I've narrowed it down to two," she says, pointing at two shades of yellow.

I look at the samples. "So, it's between dog pee and cat vomit."

"Jason. Pick up the couch." Dad now grinds his teeth. If Tony and Doreen weren't there I know he would have really lit into me.

I look over at my car. It takes all I have not to go there, but I know if I left, it would be worse when I came back.

Besides. I have nowhere to go.

But what I also wanted to do right then was interior decorate our whole living room. Decorate it quite beautifully with black spray paint. Beautify the entire room. In huge letters it would say SPIDER over the fireplace and SPIDER on the wall between the living room and dining room and SPIDER on every window so you couldn't even see out! Ha! That's some interior decoration for you.

"I'll be in as soon as we load this," Dad called to Doreen, who headed back to the house.

"Pick up the couch, Jason."

"Okay, okay." I bent over next to him and got my hands under the friggin' couch.

"Come on, Jason, we've got to lift this end up and rest it on the floor of the truck. Ready?" Dad got under the couch like he was lifting weights. I pulled my side up, although it was still not even close to the floor of the truck.

"Can't you get it higher?" Dad grunted.

"Maybe I should trade places with Jason," Tony called from his end.

"Jason just needs to work on his noodle muscles. Maybe you can use Josh's weights after he moves in." Dad laughs like he thinks this is funny. What I think would be funny would be to drop the couch on his head.

As we were getting the couch in the truck, I looked in there and it made me sick. Every piece of furniture from our living room was piled in that truck; the chairs, tables, lamps—everything!

I let go of the couch and I'm out of there. I get my books from my car and head for the house, not bothering to look back.

In the kitchen I went through the mail. Our mail slot is next to the back door and we always leave it on the counter. There are a lot of magazines and bills and a bunch of catalogs all addressed to Mom. Her name must be on every catalog list in the country; she's a real catalog queen. Dad has tried to get them to stop coming but no one seems to have paid much attention to him. But then I find gold in the middle of all the junk mail: a letter from Thao. The first good thing that has happened today.

"Jason?" Doreen calls to me from the living room. I didn't feel like answering so I just pretended I didn't hear her. I grabbed the letter and left for my room, but she comes in and blocks the stairs down to the basement.

"Jason," she says, handing me a business card, "this is the tux shop where my three J men are going to get fitted." She laughs. "You know I just love it that you all have the same initials. Jack, Jason, and Josh. It's a good sign, I just know it!"

"What's this for?" I look at the card.

"This is where we're getting the tuxes for the wedding. The fitting is Saturday any time after one o'clock."

"I'm supposed to go there this Saturday?"

"Yes. It doesn't matter what time just as long as you make it this Saturday afternoon before they close."

"When do they close?"

"Oh, I'm glad you asked. I didn't think to check, I've got so much on my mind." She smiles. "It's probably five or six. But I'll call them and let you know."

For a minute I just stare at her, wondering what this pudgy woman with her yellow paint samples is doing in my house.

"The wedding's in just three weeks, and there's a ton of things to do. But you know, Jason, if we all pitch in we can get everything done."

"Yeah," I mumble. Then I stuff the card in my pocket and go down to my room.

Fred was waiting for me. Usually he's at the kitchen door when I come home, but I guess with Dad and Tony moving everything out, Fred decided to hide in my room. I shut the door and knelt down and patted him. "It's okay, Fred. They can paint the whole house the color of cat vomit if they want, but there's no way I'll let them come in here."

I lay down on my bed and looked at the envelope of Thao's letter. Her handwriting was so nice, with each letter carefully formed. It reminded me of the times at Bertha Jane's when I helped her with her work for school. She tried so hard, wanting to do everything right. And she'd get upset when she made a mistake. Not just frustrated, but really upset. I remember telling her that Bertha Jane said learning something means you don't already know it, because you're learning. "You're not supposed to get things right the first time, Thao. All you're supposed to do is try the first time, and then practice and do it over a bunch of times. That's how you learn it. If you got it right the first time it means you already knew it and that wouldn't be learning." She would smile every time I said that. Her smile was so beautiful, it always knocked me out and I could almost see her smiling face as I opened the letter.

> Dear Jason,
>   Thank you for the letter. Thank you for telling me what is in your heart about marriage of your father. I would feel sad if my father marry someone who is not my mother. Everyone wants mother and father together. Please always tell me what is in your heart. I also have many things I tell only to you. Things I not tell Auntie. Auntie Nu-Anh is very nice, but she not know about school where I go. At school many girl have boyfriend. Even girls from Vietnam have boyfriend and they do not tell parent. Auntie Nu-Anh not know about that. I have some friends now in this school. They are Chao-Pin and Jenny in ESL class, both are very nice. They both have boyfriend but parent do not know. They say Li a boy in this class like me. This make me feel strange. It make me wish to talk to Miss Bertha Jane Fillmore. Please write to me and tell what you think. Li wants me to go his house after school. He says no one home. My friend say to tell Auntie I must do work at school to stay late there. That is what they tell parent. I have no one to tell this, Jason. Only you. Please write to me.
>   Love from your friend,
>   Thao

My stomach scrunched up when I came to the line "they say Li a boy in this class like me," and when I came to the end of the letter it was in a big knot. I threw down the letter. *What am I? Dear Abby?* Well, that's easy enough. I'll give her some advice. I got down on the floor and crawled around trying to find my notebook. I must have gotten a little wild, frantically throwing everything around looking for the sucker, because Fred leaped on my bed to get out of the way. Finally, I found it under a greasy pizza box. I tore it open and ripped out a piece of paper. Then I grabbed a pen from my desk and wrote my answer.

> Dear Thao,
> The guy's an animal. Don't go near him.
>> Love,
>> Jason

I didn't have any envelopes in my room but I didn't want to go upstairs to find one since Doreen was probably still twitting around my living room with her paint samples. She was probably going to turn our house into a clown house like her place. Well, one thing was for sure. There was no way she was going to paint my room. I would not let her pudgy self and her paintbrush anywhere near my stuff.

I put on my Discman and read Thao's letter again. Then I read mine. And right then and there Bertha Jane got in my brain again. I could hear her voice; even the old rap I was listening to wouldn't drown it out. "Jason, when we really care for someone we try to put our own feelings aside and think of the other person and what they need from us at the time."

I don't know how Bertha Jane gets in my brain like that. It sometimes seems a little spooky to me but usually I have a calm feeling inside when I imagine her talking to me. I can almost see her face and each time it's like she's with me. And usually she is with me trying to keep me from doing some crummy thing to someone.

I tore up my letter to Thao and tried to think of what the best thing would be to tell her. As I went to my notebook to get another piece of paper, I heard Doreen's heels clicking across the kitchen floor above my room and I grabbed the phone. The hell with writing. I wanted to talk to Thao. Luckily she answered and not her aunt, and I almost melted when I heard her soft voice say "hello."

"Thao, it's Jason."

"Oh, Jason. Great. I'm so happy you call me."

"I got your letter."

"Yes. Good."

"Are you okay, Thao?"

"Yes. Okay. But I don't know what to do."

"About that guy?"

"Yes. Li."

Tell the creep to hit on somebody else.

"Jason? Are you there?"

"Yeah. I was just thinking about your situation. Guess your aunt is too strict, huh?"

"Everyone I know, the parent too strict. So kids just do things anyway."

So do things with your girl friends, just stay away from guys. They're all dogs.

"Jason? You're so quiet."

"Well, I was just thinking, that's all."

"I wish I knew what Miss Bertha Jane Fillmore would tell me. . . . Jason? You there?"

"I think I know."

"What, Jason? Tell me."

"Well, I think she would ask you if you like this boy."

"I would say maybe. I don't know. He is very good-looking. Girls in ESL are crazy about him."

He's an animal! Stay away from the diphead!

"Jason?"

"Just thinking some more."

"Tell me more, okay? More what you think Miss Bertha Jane Fillmore would say."

"Okay."

"Jason?"

"Okay, she would say that if you find him attractive it would be good to get to know him and find out what kind of a person he is. Bertha Jane always thought friendship was the most important thing."

"What about going to his house?'

"She'd probably say to visit him with one of your girl friends and to tell your aunt about it."

"Oh, Jason, great. You help so much. Thank you, Jason.

"Sure."

"Jason, you okay? You sound like you have cold or something."

"Allergies. Makes my throat weird and my voice funny."

"Jason. Call me again, okay?"

"Okay."

"I miss you, Jason. . . . Jason? You still there?"

"I miss you, Thao."

"Your allergy okay? You sound strange."

"I'm okay. I better go."

"Thank you, Jason. You help me. Just like before."

"Anytime, Thao."

I got off the phone and put my Discman back on. Tears stung my eyes. I was allergic all right, allergic to the idea of Thao with somebody else. It made me sick.

 Five

I DIDN'T NEED TO drive Josh to school anymore because the coach decided it would help bring Josh up to speed if he had more time with him. So not only was Mr. Williams bringing Josh home after practice, but he was picking him up and taking him to school in the morning, like his own private chauffeur. No wonder they say those guys in the NBA are spoiled! Probably from high school on they have people waiting on them hand and foot, treating them like kings.

And not only was Josh getting special treatment from Mr. Williams but the girls in our school went berserk about the guy. His first day had been only a sample of what was to come. My chemistry class was down the hall from his French class, and that was the only time I ran into him during the day, but believe me it was enough. This is what I saw each day of the week:

Monday: Josh comes down the hall with Lauren Davis
                     and Micalea Teo, seniors who are on the cheer

	squad. At lunch he is with Molly Sturges, the homecoming queen.
Tuesday:	Josh comes down the hall with the Chan twins, Vera and Verna; they're in my class, juniors. They model for Nordstrom's. Need I say more?
Wednesday:	Josh stops at a locker. Kimberly Cotton's locker, who is there squishing her body into his.
Thursday:	Josh comes down the hall with Peggie McKee. I think she's a sophomore, but I'm not sure. All I know is she is fine.
Friday:	Josh is leaning against Kimberly Cotton's locker and she is practically drooling on him.

It would have been a lot better if the one class I had near Josh's was fifth or sixth period. But unfortunately my chemistry class was first period, and starting the morning seeing him with the finest girls in the school was enough to ruin my whole day. And if that weren't enough, it got even worse the next Monday morning when the *Ingraham High Rocket* was delivered to my homeroom.

There was his face, plastered on the front page with the headline JOSH KEMPLE NEWEST HOOP STAR! All across my homeroom newspapers rustled as everyone stared at his photo, even the guys, who said stuff like, "Hey, maybe we'll take Metro this year."

But most of the noise was girls.

"Is this guy fine, or what?"

"He looks like Leonardo DiCaprio!"

"Oh my God, he does!"

Then they read the interview with him, and it says that he moved here because his mother is getting married to Jason Kovak's dad. Twenty-nine heads, as if they are synchronized, turn to the back of the room where I sit in the last row. Everyone stares at me. Do you think I have ever been mentioned in this paper before? Even once my entire high-school career . . . freshman, sophomore, or this year, my junior year? No, I have not. Count 'em. It's three years that I've been going to this school and not once has my name ever seen the light of print in the *Rocket*. And the *Mercer Mercury*, our middle-school paper, do you think my name ever showed up there? No, it did not.

"Great about your stepbrother, Kovak." Roger Lewis waved the paper from across the room.

"Maybe he'll play for the Huskies," Chris Sturgis joined in.

"He'll be the next Detlef Schrempf," Debbie Query added her two cents.

"Hey, is he available?" Dorothy Johnson wanted to know.

"He's got a girlfriend in Chicago," I said, emphatically.

"So? She's not here, right?" Debbie laughed.

"Long-distance relationships never last. Everyone knows that." Chris gazed at his picture. "I can't get over this guy. He looks exactly like Leo."

"Hey, Jason. Does he really look like his picture here?" Dorothy asked and suddenly the eyes of every girl in the room were on me.

No. He looks like Ed, hippo at the Woodland Park Zoo. The picture's a fake.

"Well, does he?"

"Jason?"

Amazing, having these girls waiting breathlessly for my answer, their eyes all riveted on me. Every day must be like this for Josh. A person could get high on this! What a rush!

"Jason! Tell us!"

If only I could say something so funny or interesting or cool that they'd forget about him and just want to talk to me. But it was hopeless. As usual, whenever there was any pressure my mind went blank. Zero, zip, nada. Nothing.

"Yeah," I mumbled. "He looks like that."

They all went back to looking at the paper and talking about the game coming up this weekend and how they couldn't wait to see him play. I was history. That was it: my five seconds of homeroom fame when every girl in the room gave me her undivided attention and I confirmed that my stepbrother-to-be really looked like the picture in the paper. Pathetic.

That afternoon when I got home from school there was a van parked in our drive and I had to park in the street. Fred was sitting out front, and before I'd even shut off the engine, he leaped off the steps and tore across the yard to the car. The second I got out, he jumped all over me. I bent down and scratched his ears and put my cheek against his head for a minute. Fred licked my face, slobbering and wiggling around; it was like he hadn't seen me in months. He's usually happy to see me when I get home, but this was extreme.

On my way to the house, as I passed the van in the drive, I saw a bunch of ladders sticking out of it. When I opened the front door, I smelled paint and heard music, Ma$e blasting away.

"Hi. You live here?" A tall, skinny guy with a ponytail and a tattoo on his arm leaned down from a ladder. There were canvas tarps covering the floor and the living room was being transformed into a sea of cat-pee yellow.

"Yeah. Jeez, that color!"

"What?"

"Turn down the sound." A second guy painting the corner turned around. He was short and had on a Mariners cap with yellow cat-pee paint splattered on it.

"I'm up here, man."

The short guy put down his brush with a sigh, like he was really going out of his way, and walked over to the radio.

"Thanks." The ponytail guy waved his brush toward the short guy, then he looked over at me. "What were you sayin'?"

"I said, 'What a color.' "

"We don't pick 'em, man, we just paint 'em." Then he looked at Fred, who was leaning against my leg with his tail between his legs. "That dog's been freakin' out, howling and stuff."

"We didn't hurt him or nothing." The one with the cap waved his paintbrush toward Fred. "I like dogs."

"He'll be okay, now that I'm home." I leaned over and patted him. "Come on, Fred. Let's go. It stinks in here."

Fred's tail was still between his legs as he followed me down to my room. I shut the door behind us, then went over to the window and opened it as wide as it could go.

"It's okay, Fred." I pulled him up on my bed. "It's just paint. It won't hurt you."

I could hear the guys' radio blasting and their footsteps upstairs and I wanted to dump the paint cans on their heads and kick them the hell out of my house. With every footstep I felt my blood boil. "Come on, Fred. We're getting out of here." Fred jumped off the bed and I grabbed my jacket and went over to shut the window. Then the phone rang. Fred leaped back on the bed.

"Jason? It's Kimberly."

"Hi."

"Do you have a minute?"

"Sure." I sat on my bed next to Fred, scratching his ears, wondering why she called.

"Well, I guess you know about me and Kenny."

"Yeah."

"I'm kind of single now, I guess you'd say."

"What about the guy from Franklin?'

"It didn't work out."

"Oh."

"And that's why I'm calling."

"I suppose you want me to find out if Kenny's still mad?"

"I do want you to find something out for me. But not about Kenny."

"About who?"

"Josh."

About who? Right. Like you were clueless. Only every girl in the school's been hot after his butt all week.

"Jason? Are you there?"

"Yeah."

"Well, I was wondering if you knew whether or not Josh had a date for the Tolo?

"Huh."

"Jason?"

"Huh?"

"The Tolo. Does Josh have a date?"

"I dunno."

"Well, I'm thinking about asking him, but I just wanted to make sure he wasn't already going. Could you find out for me?"

"I dunno. I mean, I don't think . . ."

"Just try, okay? Thanks, Jason."

Click.

I stared at the phone and put the receiver back. Kimberly Cotton must be out of her mind. Here she goes and dumps my best friend, and then turns around and expects me to help get her together with Josh. That girl's got some kind of nerve. I really wish I'd told her to forget it, but she took me by surprise and I'm no good at thinking on my feet. It seems like I always get ideas about what I should have said when it's too late.

I sat on my bed and looked at the phone. *Maybe it wasn't too late.*

"Fred," I said, "everything is messed up around here and I haven't had anything to say about any of it. But you know what?"

Fred looked at me. I was sure he was thinking 'what?' "

"At least I don't have to help Kimberly Cotton do Kenny any worse than she already has."

Her phone number must still be in my backpack. I found it and called her back. Right away (before I'd lost my nerve).

"Kimberly? This is Jason."

"That was quick!" She laughed.

"Don't ask me to do this stuff. Kenny's my friend, just ask Josh yourself."

"Well, if that's the way you feel about it, Jason."

"That's it."

"Okay."

"So long, Kimberly." Upstairs I could hear the painters clunking around and I slammed the phone down. *Clunk.*

When I got off the phone I felt like I'd gotten food poisoning from talking to Kimberly and I needed something to heal my pain.

Not something: someone. And not just anyone, I wanted to call Thao. I'd been missing her and also worrying a lot about what had happened with her and that guy, but I'd been working on convincing myself that everything was probably okay.

The way I figured it, she had most likely gone to see that guy with a friend and he'd tried to jump on both of them, showing his true colors to be the animal we all know he is, and Thao would have hit him over the head with her purse, while her friend kicked him in the groin and then they both fled from his evil house.

I remembered the first time I saw Thao, after I answered Bertha Jane's ad in the paper. It had said, "Consultant desired for position of importance," and it was in the personal column by mistake. I didn't know what I might be getting into. The day I went there for the interview I sat parked outside in the rain, trying to get up the nerve to go in. Bertha Jane's house was huge and it had seen its better days; it was pretty run-down. I started thinking it was Norman Bates's house and I was getting creeped out. When I finally made myself go to the front door, I braced myself for Norman or some other murderer to open the door, but when it opened, there was the most beautiful girl I think I had ever seen. An Asian girl with honey skin and eyes like midnight. It was Thao Nguyen, and she and Bertha Jane changed my life.

But right now I felt like I was back at square one. Whatever confidence I had gained from the time I spent with them seemed to have gone right down the toilet with a giant flush. A giant flush called Josh Kemple.

"Hello?"

"Hi, Thao."

"Oh, Jason. Great."

Thao's voice was soft and sweet and I could picture her smiling. "How're you doing, Thao?"

She laughed. "Jason, I think you're like my brother. You call to see if I went to the guy's house?"

"Well, did you?"

"Yes."

"Well?"

"He's a nice guy."

"Oh."

Upstairs the radio had been turned off and I heard the door slam. Then I heard footsteps, big heavy ones.

"Jason, you there?"

"Yeah. I think my dad's home."

"You need to say good-bye?"

"Maybe. I dunno."

"Jason, how is it going for you?"

"Shitty," I mumbled.

"Pretty? Things are pretty good?"

"No, they're pretty bad actually."

"What happened?"

I patted Fred, not knowing what to say. Not knowing how to tell her that my house was painted the color of cat pee, our furniture was gone, this lady and her Leo-like NBA contender kid were moving in, that my cyberdate had been grounded, my best friend dumped and his former girlfriend was hot for my almost stepbrother and that right now life seemed as significant as mouse turds.

"JASON!" Dad's voice boomed from upstairs.

I covered the receiver. "I'm on the phone!"

"WELL, GET OFF! WE'RE GOING OUT TO DINNER!"

"Thao, I've gotta go."

"Thanks for calling me."

"Sure, Thao."

"Jason, I worry that you're okay?"

"I'll be okay. Don't worry."

"Write me, please."

"I will. Bye, Thao."

Nice Guy. The last thing I wanted to hear.

I thought I had accepted the fact that Thao and I would only be friends. Bertha Jane had explained all that to me when I asked Thao to go to the homecoming dance last year. Bertha Jane said Thao was trying to behave the way her parents would want her to,

even though her parents were in Vietnam. It was important for her
to honor them or something like that and in Vietnam girls her age
didn't date. And when they finally did go out with a guy, the family
had to know him. And although Bertha Jane didn't spell it out, it
was pretty clear her family only wanted her to be with a Vietnamese
boy. Not some wild American boy who would love her and leave
her—a wild man who ravages all the ladies, a wild man like Jason
Kovak. Yeah, right.

So now she'd gone over to this guy's house. Some guy in her
ESL class and it's probably a good bet he's Vietnamese and her auntie
would eventually let her have a relationship with him. Another pile
of mouse turds along the trail of my life.

Hog turds would be more accurate.

"JASON!"

"Okay, okay. I'm coming."

Dad was in the kitchen inspecting the paint. "Look at these
splatters, I swear people just don't take pride in their work anymore."

"What was wrong with the old color?"

"Fresh paint, a fresh start."

"I liked the old color."

"Come on, we've gotta get going. Our reservations are at six."

"Where?"

"We're meeting Doreen and Josh at Etta's."

"Why not La Medusa!"

"We thought it would be more of a celebration to get out of the
neighborhood, show Josh more of the city."

I didn't say a word all the way downtown. Etta's was my mom's
favorite restaurant. They made salmon with some special spice on it
and she had it every time we went there. We used to go there a lot;
it was like it was our place. But after she moved out, Dad and I
started going to this great restaurant in our neighborhood, La Medusa. It was my favorite place to eat and I couldn't see why we had
to go anywhere else just because of Josh and Doreen Kemple.

The trail of my life was now filled with cow pies.

• • •

"Hey, we lucked out!" Dad spotted a parking space a block from Etta's. "It's tight, but I think I can make it." Dad pulled in front of the space and craned his neck, looking over his shoulder, concentrating as he eased the car back and parked just inches from the curb. "Not bad, huh?" He grinned, pulling on the emergency brake and turning off the ignition. He probably wanted me to agree, but I looked out the window.

"Know what else we lucked out on, Jason?"

"Guess you'll have to tell me."

"Are you being sarcastic?"

"No. I dunno what else we lucked out on, so tell me."

"On Josh. We lucked out on Josh. Alvin Pederson at work was telling me that he has a stepkid who's on drugs, always in trouble. It's a real nightmare. And here we are with Josh, not only a nice kid, but I mean he might actually make it to the NBA!"

I got out of the car and slammed the door. Dad kept babbling on about how the college scouts were coming around to check out Josh. "Kentucky, now that'd be something. Of course Doreen would probably like it if he stayed in the Northwest. Although Husky basketball hasn't been that great, except we did produce Detlef Schrempf." On and on he went about what college he thought Josh should play for, the pros and cons of each one, yabbity-yabbity-yabbity as if I gave a flying fig.

"Take my word for it, he'll be the next Christian Laetner or maybe Vin Baker."

As we walked to the restaurant we passed a street musician on the corner, an old guy with a harmonica playing blues. He had gray hair, just a little wiry fringe around his bald head, and a face like a walnut, brown and wrinkled, like he'd spent a lot of his life outdoors, maybe riding trains and sleeping under the stars. With him was a tan, short-haired, medium-size dog that had white feet. And the dog had a little red scarf, like a bandanna, tied around his neck. The guy was playing "Mr. Bo Jangles" and dancing around, and the dog got

up on his hind legs and danced, too. I thought it was very nice and
I would have preferred hanging on the corner with this guy and his
dog than going into Etta's.

It seemed like being a street musician would be a pretty good
life. I glanced at the hat on the pavement where people tossed money.
There were just a few coins in there. But I knew it was better for
business if they didn't have a lot of cash showing, so I'm sure he
pocketed it on a regular basis. With a job like that you could work
outside, meet all kinds of people. As we went into Etta's, I wasn't
thinking about our stupid dinner, I was wondering if Fred could
learn to dance like that guy's dog.

As soon as we got in the restaurant, there were Doreen and Josh,
waiting right by the front desk. She hugs Dad, hugs me, and I start
to choke on her perfume. Dad pumps Josh's hand, whaps him on
the back; it's like no one had seen each other in five years or something. Josh and I are the only ones who just say "hi."

At dinner I study the menu. Hide behind it is more like it, so
I don't have to make conversation. I also glance out the window,
trying to see the guy and his dog, but they are around the corner
out of sight.

It didn't make any sense what I decided to order, the spice-
rubbed salmon. I mean it's not weird to order salmon there, it's
delicious. It's just that Mom seems to have forgotten I exist and so
you'd think that I wouldn't order her favorite thing.

I was the last one to order. "I'll have the spice-rubbed salmon."

"Very good," the waiter says.

"It was my mom's favorite," I say.

Then there is silence and I hum a little of "Mr. Bo Jangles" and
sip my water.

Josh turns to me. "What's a Tolo?"

My chance to be an authority (even though I have never been to
one). "It's a dance but the girls ask the guys."

"I've been to schools where the girls ask guys, they just don't
call it that."

"It's a Seattle thing. It started with some event at the University of Washington and then I guess high schools picked up on it."

"It's formal?"

"Yeah, usually a tux."

"Don't forget your tux fittings for the wedding," Doreen chirps. "When is it again, honey?"

"Anytime Saturday after one."

"Could I wear the same one to the Tolo?"

"Now there's a practical mind for you." Dad grins at Josh. "You should check that out, maybe you could get a deal."

Then the waiter came with a bottle of wine for Dad and Doreen and Cokes for me and Josh. Dad tasted the wine and when his glass and Doreen's had been filled, he clinks his glass with his spoon, like he was at a banquet trying to get the attention of the crowd, which was stupid because Josh and I were sitting there not saying anything anyway.

"I have an announcement to make."

Now what? There'd been more than enough announcements lately as far as I was concerned. Beam me up, Scotty, I'm sure I don't want to hear this.

"I want you all to know that Kovak Kans is making an official offer of employment to Josh Kemple. And our offer has flexible hours so that he can work around his basketball schedule."

"Jack, that's great!" Doreen toasts and takes a sip of her wine. "Josh had been hoping to earn some money here."

"Thanks." Josh raises his glass to Dad. "I had a pretty flexible job in Chicago but I didn't think I'd find time to look here for a while yet, I've been so busy getting up to speed with Mr. Williams."

"We'll just work around your schedule, Josh." Then Dad raises his glass again. "At Kovak Kans we know a winner when we see one." Dad grins at Josh. "And we want winners on our team!"

I sit there like I am invisible to them, wishing I could be out on the street with the Bo Jangles guy and his dog.

The trail of my life is now filled with elephant dung.

 Six

WAS TRYING TO FIND a tie. What I really wanted was a scarf, but I didn't have anything like that, so I decided a tie was the next best thing. I don't get dressed up much and only have a couple of ties. I can't even remember the last time I wore one, but finally I found this navy blue tie with ducks on it. Very preppy, I don't know what it is about preppy stuff and ducks, but preppies seem to like to decorate with ducks. I looked at the tag on the back. It was from Abercrombie and Fitch and then I remembered where I got the thing. It was from Mom's boyfriend, the one she had when she first left Bob Scanlon. He gave it to me for my birthday or Christmas, I couldn't remember which.

I pulled it out of the mess at the bottom of my closet and sat on the floor next to Fred. Fred was lying down and I had to pull him up and make him sit still while I put the tie on him. I wrapped it around his neck and then tied a big floppy bow.

"You look great, Fred. Better than if we had a scarf."

Then I went to my desk where I'd put a box of dog treats,

Original Milk-Bone Flavor Snacks. The box showed little pictures of the flavors: bacon, liver, cheese, meat, milk, poultry, and vegetable, and on the back there was a picture of Snoopy saying, "Milk-Bone is the best way to say you love your dog! Milk-Bone Flavor Snacks provide seven of your dog's favorite flavors in crunchy biscuits he craves!"

I couldn't tell what the flavors were, all the biscuits seemed to be various shades of brown. I picked one that was kind of a reddish brown, hoping that it was liver or bacon and not vegetable because I didn't think I could teach Fred to dance by motivating him with a vegetable biscuit.

"Okay, Fred, now stand up when I hum."

I held the biscuit up and instead of getting up on his hind legs, Fred just stared at the biscuit.

"Up, Fred!"

"Woof!" Fred looked at the biscuit and barked.

I decided to try and hold him up on his hind legs to see if he would get the idea.

"Okay, Fred, see? Like this."

As I was lifting up his front paw, the door to my room flew open. "Jason!"

"What?"

Dad barged in waving a paper around. "Look at this! Just look at it!"

"What?"

Then he saw Fred. "What the hell are you doing, Jason?"

"It's an experiment."

"What? Why's he wearing that tie?"

"It's to see if you can teach an old dog new tricks."

Dad looked at me and shook his head. Then he let out a deep sigh. But it was only a second before he was waving the paper around again. "The phone bill came today! Just look at these calls to California!" He holds the bill with one hand and points and jabs at it, then he shoves the bill under my nose.

"I'm not paying for this, Jason! You are!"

"Okay, okay."

"Yeah, you say 'okay, okay' but I don't see you out there pounding the pavements trying to get a new job. What I see is you dressing up the damn dog!"

"Fred's not a damn dog."

"And it's not like you don't have an opportunity. I've told you, you can work at Kovak Kans whenever you want."

"I'll find my own job."

"Yeah, well at least Josh isn't too proud to work for a portable toilet company."

"It's not the toilets!"

"Well then, what is it?"

"I don't want you for a boss! You boss me too much anyway!"

"Because you need it, Jason. And you need to get a job!" Dad stormed out and slammed the door so hard my Third Eye Blind poster fell off the wall.

I heard him stomping around upstairs, then I heard the side door slam, then I heard the garage door go up.

"Well, at least it's just us, Fred."

I decided to give Fred quite a few of the flavor biscuits even though we hadn't gotten too far with our dance lesson. While I was fishing some out of the box, the phone rang. I held the phone against my shoulder while I gave Fred the treats.

"Did you hear about Kimberly?" It was Kenny, sounding like he was sick or something his voice was so raspy.

"What about her?"

"She asked your stepbrother to the Tolo."

"Oh."

"And he's going with her."

"He's not my stepbrother yet."

"He will be soon, right?"

"I guess so."

"When's the wedding?"

"Saturday."

"So is the Tolo. Isn't he going to be at the wedding?"

"It's in the afternoon and it's just Dad, Doreen, Josh, me, and a judge. Then we have a fancy lunch in a private room at some hotel."

"So after the wedding he gets Kimberly and goes to the Tolo?"

"I guess."

"Well, don't you know? Don't you talk to the guy?"

"Not much—I don't know much about his situation."

"Well, you know what I think about his situation?"

"What?"

"Actually, man, you don't *want* to know," and he slams down the phone.

After Kenny and I had that conversation, I figured the last thing he'd want to do was go to the game and see Josh's debut as an Ingraham Ram. But he told me that it was important for him to be there and so he could ignore Kimberly. He wanted her to think the whole thing hadn't even phased him, that she meant nothing to him. She was just a little pimple on the smooth surface of his life.

Sometimes it still amazes me how different Kenny and I are. Since we've been in high school, it's become obvious that his way with women is radically different from mine. I have no way and he has one. Actually, I guess I've come to accept that, but the way he reacted to Kimberly and Josh floored me. If that happened to me I would find it so humiliating, I would be completely demolished. I'm not the kind of person who has any success at pretending things don't bother me. Maybe you have to be like an actor to pull that off, a creative person with a lot of nerve. If the Kimberly-Josh thing happened to me, I'd probably never get out of bed. I'd curl up in a ball, get under the covers, and live there.

But the night of the game, Kenny was psyched. It was like he was coming to play, too, he was so up for it.

We drive to the school. He jumps out of his car and we strut into the gym. (Actually, Kenny is struttin' and I'm sort of following along with my hands jammed in my pockets.) Kenny spots Sally

Kazama in the crowd and waves. "Hey, Sally, howzit goin'?" Big wave. Very cool.

We walk a little farther. He sees Cindy Lantry coming in the door on the opposite side of the gym. "Hey, Cindy, over here!"

Cindy waves and heads our way.

I look around and see Dad and Doreen on the top row near the south door, where the parents always sit. I don't wave.

Then I see Kimberly who is sitting in the second row behind the cheerleaders talking to her friends. I can tell Kenny has seen her because he stops exactly opposite from where she is sitting. He goes up to Debbie Query, who is waiting to go up into the bleachers, and he puts his arm around her. "Hey, Debbie, wassup?"

She leans into him. "Hey, Kenny. Good to see ya."

I stand there with my hands in my pockets looking at the empty scoreboard.

I climb up into the bleachers behind Kenny and Debbie just as there is a big drum roll and Joe Klein, our announcer, yells, "ALL RIGHT FANS! Let's hear it for the Ingraham Ra-a-a-a-ms!"

There is a huge cheer as the team runs in. The players are in the center of the gym waving to the crowd. Then Joe Klein announces the starting lineup. Big cheers for Maurice Brown, Dean Fletcher, Theodore Evan, and Richard Lloyd. Then Joe says, "And let's give a big Ram welcome to our newest Ram! At center . . . JOSH KEM-PLE!"

The place goes nuts. I look across at Kimberly who is jumping so much she loses her balance for a minute and falls into Norman Hugh, one of the guys on the cheer squad. He picks her up and throws her in the air. She squeals and then bounces back with the other girls in her row.

I find myself thinking disloyal thoughts of humiliation and de-feat as Josh goes to the center for the tip-off. A Ram blowout like the year the Sonics were annihilated by LA in the play-offs and only scored sixty-eight points in the whole game. May Josh's game be filled with stupid fouls, turnovers, and nothing but air balls. Maybe he'd get flattened trying to rebound and would crash to the ground like a felled tree and play no more. But I felt bad for that thought. Bertha Jane again, I suppose, getting into my brain and convincing me not to wish people harm. But air balls for sure. All over the place, air ball after air ball. The best scenario would be the team squeaking out a win in spite of a lackluster and totally disappointing performance by Josh.

But it was not to be. Josh was the star he was predicted to be and with each dazzling move Kenny and I slumped farther down in our seats. Ingraham beat Roosevelt fifty-seven to fifty-two, and twenty points of it were made by none other than my almost stepbrother and the Tolo date of Kenny's former girlfriend, the great Josh Kemple.

Kenny and I hardly spoke on the way home from the game and when we saw each other again the next day at lunch, we were both still kind of glum. We sat at a table in the corner of the lunchroom, both sort of picking at our food.

"Great game." Kenny sounded like he was speaking of the dead.

"Yeah." I tore a little piece of bread off the end of my sandwich and flicked it at him. "Two points for me, I'm hot."

Kenny grabbed a potato chip and flipped it at my face. "Newman for three. I'm smokin'."

It's hard to explain what happened next, it happened so fast. But I think this was the sequence of events. I pitched my hard-boiled egg at Kenny and he ducked and it hit Tom Neville at the table behind us. Then Tom turned around and clobbered Kenny in the back of the head with an orange. Then the whole lunchroom got into it. Jell-O salad was flying, milk got dumped on guys' heads, girls ran screaming from their tables. It was a major league, all-pro food fight.

The whole lunchroom was getting trashed and then the security guards came in with Mr. Hollingshead, the vice principal. It didn't seem to take long before they traced it to the beginning and Kenny and I were in Hollingshead's office.

"Sit down, Kovak. You, too, Newman." Mr. Hollingshead had our student record cards in front of him. "I'm putting calls in to your parents."

"Could we just have a warning or something," Kenny pleaded.

Hollingshead banged his fist on the table. "The only way to squash these food fights is with suspension."

"Suspension!" Kenny sat forward, gripping the arms of the chair. My stomach started to hurt like someone had punched me.

"You people never think of the consequences of this ridiculous behavior. We have to pay the custodial staff overtime just to clean up the lunchroom. We've had injuries from people slipping on all the goo on the floor. And the waste! Just the waste itself is a crime!" He spat out the words. "Last year when one of these ridiculous spectacles erupted, I had a student from Ethiopia ask me why the students were doing this. She had come here from a country where people were starving and it was beyond her comprehension that people here were throwing food at each other that could have fed half the families in her village."

I slumped as far down in my chair as I could, feeling like a loathsome piece of scum.

Kenny squirmed in his chair, looking at the floor.

"A parent is required to come to school on a one-day suspension." Hollingshead looked at our information cards. "Is this all correct, Kovak? The contact is Jack Kovak at Kovak Kans?"

I nodded.

"Your mother's not around?"

"No."

He turned to Kenny. "And your contacts are both Alice Newman and Milton Newman?"

"Yeah. My mom's probably easier to get than my dad."

"All right. I'll try her first." Hollingshead leaned back in his chair and folded his arms over his chest. "Your suspension begins now and you will go to the lunchroom and help the custodial staff until your parents arrive."

I felt like a worm crawling there on my belly as Kenny and I headed for the door.

"And I don't ever want to see either of your faces in this office again!"

Kenny and I didn't say much as we walked back to the lunchroom. When we got there the head custodian, Mr. Larson, glared at us like we were slime and pointed to two large push brooms and a mop and a bucket over against the wall. "Get everything off the floor before you mop," he snarled.

We got the brooms. Kenny started in the corner by the wall adjacent to the hall and I went to the opposite wall, pushing all the crap toward the huge garbage cans in the middle of the floor. Neither of us spoke. At the garbage can we started scooping everything up and dumping it in. I am not a squeamish person, but putting my hands in that mess was pretty yukky. I wished the custodian had given us a dustpan or something to scrape it up with, but the last thing I was going to do was ask that dude for anything.

"Newman!" Hollingshead stood in the door with Kenny's mother. "You can leave now."

Mrs. Newman works at home. She has an office in their basement, which is why she could get to school so fast. I'm not sure what she does, some kind of consulting or something. Anyway, there she was standing in the doorway of the lunchroom looking totally pissed.

"See ya, Jason," Kenny said in almost a whisper as he carried the broom and put it back against the wall and then left with his mother.

If nice Mrs. Newman was so pissed I couldn't even imagine what it would be like when Big Jack Kovak got the news. He'd go postal, the roar of his voice alone would probably shatter all the windows in the school.

Maybe I'd get lucky and Hollingshead wouldn't be able to find him. Maybe he would be out at a job and his cell phone wouldn't work and I could just spend my suspension in the lunchroom. I would just curl up in the corner next to the radiator and use my jacket for a pillow. Maybe I could sneak home and get Fred, so I'd have a little company.

I was pushing the broom back across the floor thinking about how I could work it out to get Fred when I felt the nerves across my knuckles tingle. This happens when I experience great fear. Without looking I knew he was there.

"Get over here, Jason." Dad's voice was calm but deadly. Like the way someone might say, "Ready . . . fire," right before pulling the trigger to execute some poor slob.

I took the broom back and leaned it against the wall. Dad turned to Hollingshead, who had come with him to the lunchroom. "We'll take care of this at home, you can be assured. And I'm very sorry that my son has caused this trouble." Dad was using his most polite voice, but the muscles in his neck were twitching in spasms and his face was dark pink.

"He will be allowed back on Friday. He can just go to his home-room and resume his normal schedule."

Dad didn't say a word as we left the school and went to the parking lot. We got in the car and he drove down Meridian to the freeway staring straight ahead as if he were alone in the car. I almost think his silence was worse than if he had started yelling. The tension made me want to throw up. It was like a bomb ticking.

South on I-5 to the Columbian Way exit.

Silence.

To our neighborhood.

Silence.

Down our street.

Silence.

Into the garage.

Silence.

Dad got out of the car and went into the house.

Still not a word.

I followed him in the side door and shut the door behind me.

He stood in the middle of the kitchen. "Sit down, Jason." The same deadly calm voice. *Click.* The rifle cocked and ready.

I imagined bullets whizzing by my head, wondering which one was about to hit me.

"Wait here," Dad commanded and then left the kitchen.

I looked out the window at the trees in our backyard and above them at the sky. It was bright blue with big banks of fluffy white clouds, the kind that made you want to lie on your back and look up to find things. Elephants and hippos, tugboats and ocean liners, Ferris wheels, bananas, kangaroos, unicorns, and goats, and I saw Bertha Jane's face, and I wished I could bring her here next to me and feel her love wrapped around me like a warm blanket. "You're not a criminal, Jason. The wonder is that you're doing as well as you are with all the change that's happening in your life. What happened wasn't your fault." Her voice was so sweet and kind, I felt myself relax like I was in a warm bath.

Rubber duckie, you're the one, you make bath time really fun.

Dad came back in the room carrying a large black book. Maybe it was a book of torture, a manual describing all the evil things he would do to punish me.

"This is a Bible." Dad stared at me.

I almost fell over. Dad doesn't do Bible. Mom didn't do Bible. Between him being raised Jewish and her being raised Episcopalian, Bible fell through the cracks.

"I talked to Doreen right after I got the call from Mr. Hollingshead. And she thinks you may be deliberately trying to sabotage our wedding. Which is this Saturday, in case you forgot."

"I didn't forget."

"It is beyond me why you choose to throw food instead of a basketball or baseball like a normal kid."

"What's the Bible for?"

"At the wedding you and Josh are going to read from it. And between now and the wedding, since you're suspended from school, I want you to practice your part. It's right here. Doreen's put bookmarks in the places where you are to read. It's *I Corinthians 13* and

Ecclesiastes 3. Practice saying it over and over, because we want to be able to hear you."

"That's it. I mean, that's all you have to say."

"Not quite."

I braced myself. Finally, now he would really unload. His usual barrage, exploding, ripping, tearing into me. Here it comes. . . .

"Doreen and I decided that if you don't get yourself a job and if you get into any more trouble at school, we're sending you to a psychiatrist."

So that was it. He's not yelling at me because he thinks I'm a nutcase. Dad turned and left. I heard the car start and the garage door go up and then when I knew he was gone, I went down to my room with Fred to give him the news.

I sat on my bed and Fred looked up at me with his trusting brown eyes. Fred loves me no matter what.

"He used to think I was a loser, Fred. But now he thinks I'm crazy."

📁 Seven

I GOT AROUND TO LOOKING at the Bible the day before the wedding. I leafed through it and opened it to the first bookmark, a sheet of note paper from Doreen's travel agency. HAPPY HOLIDAYS! FOLLOW YOUR DREAMS WITH US ran across the top, next to the logo. Their logo was a fluffy cloud with "H H" perched on it with little colored dots all around. It looked like it could be acid rain or a hailstorm but I guess it was supposed to be confetti to go with the holiday idea. The address, phone, fax, E-mail and Web site were printed in curly letters that were probably meant to look dreamy, but there were so many swirls it was kind of hard to make it out, especially the Web site. Looking at the bookmarks, it was obvious that choosing what to read at the wedding was Doreen's project. I would bet anything Dad didn't even know what was in the Bible.

The Bible itself seemed stiff as I opened it. I held it up to my nose and smelled it, and it definitely smelled new. I was quite sure it was, since I didn't think we owned one and even if Doreen did, she probably wanted to get a new Bible especially for the wedding. Smelling new books was something I got from Mom. She always did that. She said there was something special about the smell of a new book. Her favorite books were big ones with glossy color pictures. Books on furniture over the centuries, fancy gardens, interior design, flower arrangements. She always had a book of this type on the coffee table.

I read the first passage silently. Then two more times after that to myself before I decided I was ready to read it to Fred and pretend he was a guest at the wedding.

"Listen up, Fred. I'm going to read from a very important book. The Bible. So don't fool around. Pay attention." Even though I was just reading to Fred, it still made me nervous and I don't think I would have felt that way if I was reading him an item from *Sports Illustrated* or the newspaper. I stood with my back to my computer, holding the Bible out in front of me opened to the first HAPPY HOLIDAYS bookmark. Fred sat about three feet in front of me, looking up curiously while his tail thumped the floor. This was a little distracting, but I would never want to tell Fred not to wag his tail. That just wouldn't be right, so I looked at him, cleared my throat, and began:

> For everything there is a season and a time for every matter
>   under heaven
> A time to be born, and a time to die;
> A time to plant, and a time to pluck up what is planted;
> A time to kill, and a time to heal;
> A time to break down, and a time to build up;
> A time to weep, and a time to laugh;
> A time to mourn, and a time to dance;
> A time to throw away stones, and a time to gather stones
>   together;
> A time to embrace, and a time to refrain from embracing.
> A time to seek, and a time to lose;
> A time to keep, and a time to throw away;

A time to tear, and a time to sew;
A time to keep silence, and a time to speak;
A time to love and a time to hate;
A time for war, and a time for peace.

The passage I read was also kind of confusing to me. I didn't know much about what was in the Bible and it surprised me that it said there was a time for killing. Did that mean killing animals and fish for food? Or did it mean killing people? I thought the Bible was supposed to help people be good? Oh well, it wasn't my wedding, if they wanted me to read that, it was up to them. And at least they'd planned it to be small, it was going to be a midget wedding with only four people: Doreen, Dad, Josh, me, and the judge. It was also going to be outside in the University of Washington Arboretum, which would make it a lot more casual than having it at a church with a big crowd invited, like everyone from Kovak Kans. I'd hate to have to read the Bible at a huge thing like that.

I opened the Bible to the next HAPPY HOLIDAYS bookmark. There was a little yellow Post-it in the margin with arrows pointing to different parts of the text, and in Doreen's writing it said, "only these verses."

I read them to myself first the way I had with the other one and then aloud to Fred.

Love is patient; love is kind; love is not envious or boastful or arrogant or rude. It does not insist on its own way; it is not irritable or resentful, it does not rejoice in wrongdoing, but rejoices in the truth. . . . Now faith, hope, and love abide, these three, and the greatest of these is love.

This seemed better than the one that mentioned there was a time to kill. I was still quite surprised by that; in fact, I would really like to discuss it with someone. But the only person I could think of who you could talk with about this kind of thing was Bertha Jane. The second reading made me think about Bertha Jane, too, and miss her because it seemed like something she might say, in regular words of course. She was that kind of a person. I read it again.

Love is patient . . .

I closed the Bible. "You know, Fred, I have been quite patient waiting for love, to tell you the truth, and it's getting pretty hard to keep being patient." Fred's tail thumped the floor. I set the Bible on my desk and I looked at the calendar where I'd circled the date when Allison Gray was through being grounded. It would be next week. Good, I thought, I wouldn't have to wait that much longer.

I went to my computer and turned it on. "Might as well practice some brilliant chatter in a chat room, Fred. So I'll be ready for my private chats with Allison." I patted Fred's head and scratched his ears (which he loves) while I got on-line and went into a chat room.

You have just entered room "Town Square—bestlilchathouse 6."

Emanon8:	What's her name?
Gumby73333:	17/m here
Mickey1317:	wassup yall
WATER4T99:	Well this KALI girl is cutting to IM have FUN!!
HEERZ2U:	age/sex/loc check
Emanon8:	Where are the girls?
Nater16:	Eat #@!*
Mickey1317:	16f/PA
Emanon8:	VA
HEERZ2U:	age/sex Emanon?
Mickey1317:	U Heerz? age/sex
Nater16:	I'VE BEEN HIGH.#$@'D ALL THAT GOOD STUFF
HEERZ2U:	I'm about to get high
Emanon8:	Hey, where are the girls?
Mickey1317:	ne 1 from chi?
Mayhem567:	Age/sex/place check . . . please???
Nater16:	Come smoke with me Heerz

Mickey1317:	Bulls rule losers
Mayhem567:	you have mail
Emanon8:	Hey, where are the girls?
HEERZ2U:	lol
Mickey1317:	15/f/IL

(This is where I decided to jump in.)

JayKae:	Love is patient; love is kind
Emanon8:	Hey, where are the girls?
Nater16:	I SAID Come smoke with me Heerz IM me
Mickey1317:	Hey peeps—ne 1 from chi?
JayKae:	love is not envious or boastful or arrogant or rude
HEERZ2U:	whooz rude dude?
Mayhem567:	You have mail
JayKae:	It does not insist on its own way
Mickey1317:	Bulls forever! I insist JayKae!
HEERZ2U:	ur a pervert JayKae!
Emanon8:	Hey, where are the girls?
JayKae:	it is not irritable or resentful
Mickey1317:	u irritate me JayKae
JayKae:	it does not rejoice in wrongdoing
Nater16:	WHO IS THIS DIPHEAD?
Mayhem567:	Get outa the room JayKae. You have mail.
JayKae:	But rejoices in the truth
Mickey1317:	Here's the truth—JayKae u sux
Emanon8:	age/sex/place check peeps, NOW!
HEERZ2U:	JayKae is an old fart
Mickey1317:	Rejoice in this truth peeps—BULLS BULLS BULLS!
JayKae:	Now faith, hope and love abide, these three
Nater16:	GET OUT WEIRDO!
Emanon8:	He's sick, forget it, age/sex/place check Come on peeps!

JayKae:	And the greatest of these is love
WATER4T99:	Well this KALI girl is BACK!!

That seemed like a good place to quit. I was sitting there thinking about what it was about the stuff I wrote that made everyone so
mad, when a little box popped down on my screen. An instant message! It was from someone who's screen name was TIGER. My own
private little conversation . . . Great!

TIGER0368:	Hey JayKae. You write about love. How bout it?
JayKae:	How 'bout what? Age/sex check please
TIGER0368:	Want to cyber? Yes or no.
JayKae:	More details k?
TIGER0368:	Cyber sex
JayKae:	No.

Yuk. It had to be some weirdo. I quit the room and was logging
off when the little yellow envelope showed up and it said, "You've
got mail." I clicked on it and there were a bunch of E-mails all lined
up like I'd been invaded. They were from: stinlyparker7@
worldnet.att.net, hvll@mci.com, bellydncrs43@worldnet.att.net,
and bgbghg46 @londonlife.com.

I opened them and they were all from sex sites. Each message
said Adults Only (as if that's really going to stop a kid from reading
the thing—*duh*). Like swarms of locusts, they swoop into your machine and start sending you this stuff telling you they have free
pictures and then you're supposed to say you're over twenty-one and
whip out your credit card. (As I mentioned, I have been curious
about this and checked out some free pics in the past, but today to
have this junk in my machine only seconds after I quit the chat room
really made me mad.)

Enough! My school is invaded by Josh, my best friend's relationship has been invaded by Josh, my house has been invaded by
painters and also is about to be invaded by Josh and Doreen and now

to have people invading my computer is putting me on the edge of total meltdown. I'm sick of being invaded! *Enough!*

I tried to calm down by reminding myself that at least I didn't have that long to wait until Allison would be back and the Net would be fun again. But then I started to feel kind of sick. Not about the sex sites but about me.

Was I as much of a pervert as that TIGER weirdo?

That idea started to get me depressed (as if I wasn't depressed enough already). But I was sure there had to be a difference between just imagining having sex with someone (sort of dreaming about it on your own, which I did a lot of) and having cybersex with some person you found in a chat room, where you wrote sexy stuff to each other. That seemed creepy to me.

I needed to get outside and get some fresh air, so I took Fred and some stale bread and walked down to the lake to feed the birds. I stayed away from the boathouse where the Canada geese hang. Not that I don't like them, one at a time, or maybe a nice little family of three or four. But we have a whole city of them living near the boathouse on Lake Washington and they seem to be thriving just fine without my stale Bravo Bakery sourdough bread. If you fed a couple and then the bread ran out they could kill you. I'm serious. Peck you to death or something.

Usually when I feed the birds, it clears my head. But as the sparrows hopped around and a few ducks swam over, I was thinking about how nice it would be to be one of them. They don't have birds creeping out other birds wanting cybersex. They just hang together, have fun, build their little nests. Life is normal for them. They don't even have to worry about being in a wedding the next day, like I was.

Even though it was nice to think about the kind of life birds have, I didn't get completely rid of feeling creeped out, because that night, which was the night before the wedding, I had an awful dream, a nightmare where an army of sleazy people in their underwear, both men and women with greasy hair and grungy yellow teeth and warts and hairy moles on their bodies came marching out of my computer into my room. They all jumped on me and I couldn't breath. I was choking and suffocating in smelly armpits and gross rolls of fat and dirty feet.

When I woke up I felt sick. Usually, I hit the snooze alarm every five minutes for sometimes as much as forty-five minutes, but I was afraid if I went back to sleep, the dream would come back. So I got up and jumped in the shower. Most of the time I wait until the temperature is just right before I get in there, but this morning I got in as fast as I could and just let the water run all over me. I didn't care that it wasn't warm enough. Then I dumped practically the whole bottle of shampoo on my head as if a large amount of shampoo would get the disgusting people out of my brain. There was a ton of lather and I made spikes out of my hair, white soap spikes all over. I peeked my head around the curtain and looked in the bathroom mirror. It was steaming up, but I could still see how I looked with spikes, getting the idea of what platinum blond spikes might look like. I was also imagining how this might look if I added a ring in my nose when I heard banging on the door. I knew it was Dad so I reached around and opened the door, and it was Dad except that I hardly recognized him. He stood there in his tux, looking like a nightclub emcee.

"Here's yours, Jason." He held a plastic clothes bag on a hanger. "We leave in a half hour. How much longer are you going to be?"

"I'm almost done."

"I'll put the tux in your room." Dad looked at my head. "You always wash your hair like that?"

"Just for special occasions."

"Did you practice the readings?"

"Sure."

"Did you say it out loud in front of the mirror?"

"I read it to Fred."

Dad looked at my hair again and then sighed his my-son-is-a-wacko sigh. "Well, come up as soon as you're ready. A half hour, Jason."

"Okay."

• • •

Dad left and I took one last look in the mirror at my spikes before I rinsed it all off and finished showering. The clothes bag was hanging over my closet door and when I opened it, I was surprised to see how much stuff went with a tux. There were even shiny shoes in a shoe box in the bottom of the bag. I thought the black cummerbund would really look nice on Fred. It would fit perfectly around his middle and I also wanted to see if the suspenders could work as a slingshot. It might make quite a powerful one with all that elastic. But I knew I couldn't take time out for this so I just put on the tux. No fooling around. No slingshot, no cummerbund for Fred. What a good boy.

I wasn't at all ready for how I would look in the thing. After I was completely dressed—shoes, studs in the shirt, cuffs, tie, suspenders, cummerbund, the whole nine yards, I looked in the mirror and was extremely surprised. It's not that I had become a whole different guy, but I seemed older and taller and better-looking and I wished I was going somewhere besides my dad's wedding. I practiced some dance moves in front of the mirror. I was at Allison Gray's prom and we were smokin' up the dance floor. Every girl in the place couldn't wait to dance with me, but Allison was possessive.

"He didn't come all this way to dance with anybody but me!" Allison waved at her beautiful girlfriends to back off.

Then a slow dance came, and I took her in my arms.

"JASON!" Dad yelled down the stairs. "It's time!"

That cooled my jets, and I went up to the kitchen where Dad was waiting. He jiggled the car keys and tapped his foot while he stared out the window. He seemed pretty wired.

"Where's the Bible? We're using the one I gave you."

"Okay, I'll get it."

"Hurry up, I don't want to be late!"

Actually, I thought I'd grab the Bible and read the whole book while you waited up here. Man, he was some kind of uptight.

I could feel the tension vibrating off him as we drove to the Arboretum to meet Doreen and Josh. I imagined it was like electricity shooting currents out of his head in every direction. He hardly said a word to me and I didn't have anything to say to him. What was there to say? Dad thinks I'm mental and there's less hope now of him ever understanding how I feel about anything. There was more hope when he just thought I was a loser.

When we were about a half-mile from the Arboretum, he finally spoke. "Well, I guess we'd say you were the best man."

"I am?"

"Sure. You hand me the ring when the judge tells us."

"Okay."

"Might as well give it to you now." We stopped at the light on Madison and Lake Washington Boulevard and Dad unbuckled his seat belt. He reached in the pocket of his tux pants and pulled out a blue velvet box. "Don't lose it," he warned as he handed it to me.

Glad you told me that. I was about to stick my hand out the window and start juggling it.

"Put it in your pants pocket for now. Then put it in your jacket pocket when we get there."

That's good information, because I was going to wear it on my head like a little hat.

"So if I'm the best man, what does that make Josh, a bridesmaid?"

"Jason, just this once don't be a wiseass, okay?" He shot me a disgusted look.

I stared out the window at the soccer field in the Arboretum. Two little kids teams were playing. They had on nice uniforms and matching socks, one team in blue, the other in red with black stripes on the shirts. The kids in blue moved down the field bunched in a pack going toward the red team's goal. Their little arms were flailing around and every kid was trying to kick the ball, while on the sideline the parents jumped up and down, cheering and shouting to them.

Then I spot a kid on the blue team, back by the goal. He's probably supposed to be a defender, but he's sitting down. He seems to be concentrating on something, so I roll down the window and stick my head out to get a better look.

"Jason! What're you doing?" Dad pats and smoothes his hair, trying to keep it from blowing around. "Put that up!"

"Okay, okay." But I did get a better look and I see that the kid is making a mud pie. I love this kid. Go for it! Make that pie! You're a champion!

Bertha Jane would have loved this kid, too. In fact, she's just about the only person I can think of who would have appreciated him. But then I saw something on the field that got me. The kid's dad saw him and he goes charging down the side of the field like a big moose and stands across from the kid and starts screaming at him. The guy is in a rage, bellowing and shaking his fist and motioning for the kid to stand up and play. I looked away from the field. I couldn't stand it, I really couldn't.

"Did you bring the Bible?"

"You already asked me that."

"Well, read your part again, we're almost there."

"Out loud?"

"No, just go over it yourself."

I opened it and read the one at the first HAPPY HOLIDAY bookmark and then turned to the second one about love.

Love is patient;
Is Dad patient? No.
Love is kind;
Is Dad kind? Not to me lately.
Love is not envious or boastful or arrogant or rude.
Yelling at me all the time seems pretty rude.
It does not insist on its own way;
Ha! He always insists on his own way!
It is not irritable or resentful.
Lol (as they say on-line, "laugh out loud")! He's always pissed at me.

So if love is supposed to be all this stuff and Dad flunks, does that mean he doesn't love me?

"This is it." Dad swung into the parking lot near the Arboretum's Visitor Center. "You have the ring?"

No. I threw it in the bushes.

I patted my pocket. "It's here."

"Good, and the Bible."

"Relax, Dad. I got it."

He looked at me like he wasn't sure if he could believe me, even though the Bible was right there in my lap. I picked it up. "See. I got it."

"All right, let's go." He glanced at me as if I was a monkey in a third-rate circus and he wasn't sure if I'd do the act or just sit there and put sawdust on my head.

It's an awful feeling not to have someone respect you. Like the father who was screaming at his kid for making a mud pie. What kind of respect is that? Why'd he make the kid be on the team anyway? People are so stupid.

We got out of the car, Dad locked it, and we walked across the parking lot. I noticed a chickadee sitting on the branch of an evergreen at the edge of the lot and a blue stellar jay, higher up on the same tree. A few sparrows were checking out the ground around a park trash can and it made me wish I had some bread. Not many people seemed to be visiting the Visitor Center; everything was pretty quiet. As I walked next to Dad, I could hear birds chirping and the gravel crunching under our feet and then in the distance the faint sound of shouting rose up from the soccer field. Someone must have scored a goal.

Score a goal. Make 'em proud. Play to win.

"They're here." Dad spotted Doreen's car. "Hope they haven't been here long."

"We're not late, are we?"

Dad looked at his watch. "No, we're a few minutes early."

"Where are we supposed to meet them?"

"By a tree."

"Dad, there are a lot of trees in the Arboretum."

"Don't be a wiseass."

"I'm serious, which tree?"

"Don't you think I know which tree I'm going to for my own wedding?" he snapped.

The crowd from the game cheered again and I wanted to be down on the field sitting in the mud next to the kid so we could make a few pies together. Maybe even cupcakes, or some mud doughnuts.

I followed Dad to a trail at the end of the parking lot. It was narrow so I walked behind him along the trail until we got to a clearing. Doreen, Josh, and a guy with a mustache wearing a herringbone jacket were there. I guess he was the judge, because the other person who was there was a lady who wasn't too dressed up and she had a camera and a big camera bag. Doreen was wearing a fancy pink dress and was holding a bunch of flowers. Josh, of course, was towering over everyone. In his tux he looked like some star NBA guy collecting a Player of the Year award at a spectacular sports banquet.

Doreen hugged Dad and me. Cough, cough as I got squished. Dad hugged Josh, and Josh and I sort of shook hands, which seemed completely stupid. Doreen introduced us to Judge Talbot and Rosetta Taylor, the photographer.

Then the wedding started.

Here comes the bride all fat and wide.

The sun filtered down through the trees and felt warm against the back of my neck. . . . And there was Bertha Jane's voice, popping into my head. . . . "Jason, he loves you the best he can. Not everyone is equally good at loving."

I closed my eyes, trying to hold on to her.

Then it was time for my part.

I opened the Bible and read it and I didn't mess up and when I was done, Dad seemed to breathe a huge sigh of relief that I'd gotten through it and hadn't put sawdust on my head.

Josh read his stuff, and I guess it went okay, although I wasn't paying that much attention because I was watching a little spider making its way across the photographer's tan leather camera bag.

The itsy bitsy spider goes up the camera bag
When it sees the bride it really wants to gag

When I looked away from the bag, Dad was kissing Doreen and the wedding was over. Then the photographer lined us up and made us strike different poses while she shot a lot of film.

Smile. Click. One big happy family. Click. Click. Click.

Up on the rooftop click click click Down through the chimney with old St. Nick. It's Christmas in springtime in the beautiful Arboretum. Smile everybody. The family is gathered. Smile. Smile. Click. Click. Click.

I tried to get Bertha Jane's voice back instead of making up the spider song, but I couldn't seem to make it happen. It's so weird the way it works. Sometimes her voice just pops into my head and it's so real, like she's there with me. But I haven't found a way to control having her show up, the way you'd put a video in the VCR and see a film whenever you wanted. I decided I probably needed to make up spider songs to get through the rest of it. So that's what I did.

We went to Fuller's restaurant in the Sheraton Hotel where we had a private room. Dad, Josh, and Doreen did all the talking. About basketball. What else?

"You're awfully quiet, Jason." Doreen smiled at me.

"Just enjoying the food, I guess."

First course: crab, avocado, and mushroom salad.

Out came the sun and dried up all the shrooms

Entrée: salmon filet with champagne sauce.

And the itsy bitsy spider peed all over the groom

Dessert: chocolate torte with fresh strawberries and crème fraîche

The itsy bitsy spider goes up the camera bag
When it sees the bride it really wants to gag

That's as far as I got with the song. After lunch Dad and Doreen drove away in Dad's car. They were spending the night at the Inn at Ludlow Bay on the Olympic Peninsula and would be back Sunday night. This summer, they had some kind of a trip planned that would be more of a honeymoon, but I guess tonight was supposed to be a little mini honeymoon.

Josh and I waited by the front door of the hotel for the valet parking guy to bring Doreen's car.

"Got plans this afternoon, Jason?"

"Just taking the tux back."

"Okay if I move some stuff over from my mom's place?"

"Fine by me."

"She wants everything moved in by Sunday night."

"There's more? I mean, all the furniture's been moved in right?"

"Yeah, it's just clothes and stuff." Josh looked at his watch. "I hope I have time."

"For what?"

"Kimberly's pickin' me up at five for the Tolo."

"Shouldn't be a problem if you're just bringing clothes over."

"Yeah, I guess. But I just wanted to be at my mom's place for a while." Josh looked over at me but he didn't say anything.

"Well, whatever. You've got a key so just come whenever."

"Yeah. Okay. The thing is, I just really feel like calling my dad."

"Where is he?"

"Mexico City. I'm not sure what time it is there, but he doesn't care if I wake him up."

I'd like to call my mother too, except she'd probably tell me it wasn't convenient.

Hey star? And you know what else isn't convenient? Having you go to the Tolo with my best friend's girl.

And you know what else? Having you move into my house.

IT'S NOT #@%!*#@ CONVENIENT!

📁 Eight

B Y MONDAY AFTERNOON WHEN I got home from school it was official. Josh and Doreen lived in my house. At noon that day Doreen had given her key to the new owner of her condo and our house, 2939 34th Ave. S, where I had lived since I was born, was now their sole residence and permanent home. Doreen was also now officially Doreen Kovak. She explained that she was an old-fashioned person and taking Dad's name was part of her traditional family values. I didn't care what she valued or what she called herself, she could call herself Doreen the Toilet Queen for all I cared as long as she kept out of my face and left me alone.

After school, Josh was always at practice and Dad and Doreen were at work and that was the only time my house seemed normal, the way things were before the invasion. That's exactly what it felt like whenever I left my room to go upstairs: an invasion by aliens. Not only did it look different with the new weird paint and Doreen's clown furniture, but it smelled different. Doreen mentioned that she always wore the scent of her favorite flower, gardenia, and its odor now blanketed the house with its awful flowering stink.

Those few hours before they came home gave me the chance to surf the Web uninterrupted and with privacy. Most of the time I darted from chat room to chat room just reading what was going on. Every once in a while I'd jump in and say something, but it was usually asking someone where they were from and nothing that would get anyone riled up, like the stuff from the Bible. And as usual, every time I'd been in a room for more that a few minutes, I'd get tons of E-mail. The batch I got Wednesday afternoon was typical. From dibldappies@worldnet.att.net saying to "click here if you want to see some good porn, we have all kinds of chicks." Next was an E-mail from winner@netexpress.net. The heading said, "MAKE MONEY WITH YOUR HOME COMPUTER!!! LOOK AT THIS! This may be the most significant letter you receive this year!!!" Then it was two pages of crap about how you were supposed to send one dollar to the seven addresses listed below and you could get up to $800,000. You were also supposed to pay eighty-nine dollars to a bulk E-mail company and then send out the chain letter to all those people. They had a phone number of the company and so I called the number to tell them they were jerks, but the line was busy.

The next one was from giewacu75@earthlink.net.

Get The Bags Out! This Vacation Could Be Yours! Bon Voyage! You have been selected to enter a World Class Florida/Bahamas Vacation Package Offer.

Then they listed the hotels, a cruise, a free rental car and said it was a three-thousand-dollar value for only $339. It's always fishy when a company doesn't list its name and asks you to register and put in your credit card number before you get the trip. *Sure.* The next one was from 80134202@postmaster.co.uk

Affordable Family Dental Care. With over 30,000 dentists nationwide we'll have one near you. For about $10.00 your family will save an aver-

age of 30 to 80% on all dental procedures. Includes: Routine cleaning
and polishing, fillings, root canals, crowns, dentures, braces. New seal-
ants to prevent cavities. Cosmetic dentistry such as teeth whitening and
veneers. No paperwork, all pre-existing dental problems qualify with no
waiting periods. Toll-free doctor locator number.

I wasn't sure what the scam was here, but it seemed like they
wanted ten dollars a month to give you phone numbers. I thought
about calling and suggested they look for a dentist after I smashed
their mouths.

The last one was the weirdest. It was from peromones1
@mailcity.com. "Sexually Attract Women Easily" was the title, and
it got my attention.

Sexually attract women easily. Use Pheromones, an invisible, odorless,
and undetectable compound when unknowingly inhaled by an adult
woman, androstenone pheromone concentrate unblocks all restraints
and releases her raw animal sex drive! Scientists have isolated the natural human male pheromone attractants and they are NOW available to
YOU legally, in the U.S.A. Everytime you wear Androstenone Pheromone
Concentrate it will send out a natural chemical signal of sex appeal to
women that will compel them toward you, make you irresistible to
them, and they will not know why. It will miraculously increase your
sexual attractiveness with women. This in return will allow you to meet
more women than you ever imagined! Even after a small application of
Androstenone Pheromone Concentrate, you will notice women suddenly
making eye contact, flirting and walking up to you, and introducing
themselves.

You were supposed to send them $19.95 for a bottle of the stuff
and it had a "money-back guarantee if you don't notice a drastic
increase in the amount of women approaching you."

I had to admit that the idea of this thing was quite wonderful.
I knew it was another scam, but for a second I imagined putting the
stuff on and walking into my homeroom, having to fight off the

girls. The problem was, though, once I had attracted a girl, I would have to face that I have no clue what to do next. It made me wish I had gotten a book I saw called *Sex for Dummies*. I saw it in a bookstore and paced back and forth in front of it for hours, but never could bring myself to take it up to the check-out. Wimp-out King, that's me.

As I sat there in front of my computer with the Sexually Attract Women E-mail on the screen, wishing for a *Sex for Dummies* book, I suddenly got an instant message.

I glanced at the box and when I saw what it was I got so excited I screamed "YES!" and threw my arms in the air. This enthusiastic display scared Fred and he began whimpering and shaking. Poor Fred. There have been so many changes around here, I can see that he is extra sensitive to my every move.

"It's okay, Fred. My cyberpal is back. It's Allison Gray!"

I guess Fred decided everything was all right, because he stopped shaking and lay back down again by my feet. But as I read the message, I was the one who was shaking. From excitement.

Surfsup10:	Hi Jason, Wassup? i'm not grounded! it's awesome to be back on-line, believe me. We had early dismissal today so i'm here chattin' like crazy. Makin' up for lost time. r u on-line now? Let me know. Later—Allison

(Yes, I am on-line. Just sitting here reading about how to sexually attract women. Looks like just reading about Androstenone Pheromone Concentrate got results!)

JayKae:	Hey, Allison! Welcome back. I'm here, just surfin the web.
Surfsup10:	Cool. Glad u r on-line. So, what's been happening?
JayKae:	Just the usual crap. Except my Dad got married.

Surfsup10:	How wuzit? Was there a wedding?
JayKae:	Yeah.
Surfsup10:	A big one? i love weddings.
JayKae:	Just Dad, my new stepmom, Doreen, and my new stepbrother. Outside.
Surfsup10:	Outside?
JayKae:	By some trees.
Surfsup10:	Is ur stepbrother a dork like you said?
JayKae:	Not really, but just kind of average I guess.
Surfsup10:	Well, that's better than a dork.
JayKae:	I guess you cud say that. What did u do when u were grounded?
Surfsup10:	u don't wanna know.
JayKae:	y not?
Surfsup10:	2 boring.
JayKae:	I can't imagine n e thing about u is boring.
Surfsup10:	:)Thanx!
JayKae:	n e time.:)
Surfsup10:	Do u have ur pic yet, Jason?
JayKae:	Should have 1 soon.
Surfsup10:	Send it k?
JayKae:	k
Surfsup10:	i'm serious. Getting grounded has made me very demanding.
JayKae:	How demanding?
Surfsup10:	Very. Like i won't send n e more IM's unless i get a pic.
JayKae:	ur serious.
Surfsup10:	Damn right. i'm tough. lol.
JayKae:	Same game here.
Surfsup10:	Explain?
JayKae:	No more IM's unless I get a pic.
Surfsup10:	u got it. Send it tomorrow.
JayKae:	May take a day or 2.
Surfsup10:	No way. Gotta b tomorrow?

JayKae:	y?
Surfsup10:	Every 1's got a picture and if they don't send it u know ur dealing with a dog. No offense. lol.
JayKae:	Seems like u thot about this a lot. lol.
Surfsup10:	u got that right. Send ur pic tomorrow. i gotta get off. Later, Jason. Luv chattin with ya!
JayKae:	Me 2. Send ur pic tomorrow too. Time?
Surfsup10:	Next week k?
JayKae:	I ask u is that fair?
Surfsup10:	lol. No. But we're going to Kaui for the weekend and I wanna take the pics with me. I'll send mine next week Promise. k?
JayKae:	Is this some kind of contest?
Surfsup10:	Personality counts too! Later, Allison.

I logged off the Net and slumped in my chair. What was I going to do about a picture? I was pretty sure the most recent one I had was in the yearbook from last spring. It was my homeroom picture and I stood in the second row behind Tiffany Dowsing who had big hair blocking out my face from my chin to the middle of my nose.

As far as family pictures went, Mom had been the photographer at our house and there hadn't been many pictures since she left. Mom had really been into photography. She took a class and for a while went around taking black-and-white photos of everything. Flowers, fences, leaves, the sidewalk up close, fruit, the sewer drain on our street. Even the toilet brush leaning against the pipes behind the toilet, if you can believe that. Sometimes at first you didn't know what the picture was. She said she looked for art in the ordinary. During her portrait phase, she made me be the model and I had to sit by the window with a black velvet thing around my shoulders and lean against the brick of the chimney with my head next to the brick. Another time she made me put my face near a candle which almost caught my hair on fire. I never saw much art in her pictures, frankly. Once I figured out what they were, they just looked to me like blurry ordinary stuff in black and white.

The more I thought about this, the more I realized there really hadn't been one single picture Dad had taken since she left. So except for the yearbook one with Tiffany Dowsing's hair in my face, the wedding pictures would be the only recent ones. And they'd never be ready in time to send to Allison. I went upstairs to get a Coke while I thought about how to solve this picture problem.

I still haven't gotten used to our refrigerator. It is a mild shock just to open the door and find an entire new type of food there. It is filled with every kind of low-fat product imaginable. Low-fat cheese, low-fat milk, weird egg substitute stuff with no cholesterol, low-fat bacon, veggie hot dogs that look like rubber, and three kinds of diet soda. I like classic Coke, there is no alternative as far as I'm concerned, and I had to dig through all this diet junk to find one. I don't think the low-fat stuff is doing Doreen much good, or else she just eats a ton of it so it doesn't count, because her resemblance to Miss Piggy remains quite strong.

After I found my can of classic Coke, I stood in the doorway of the living room just shaking my head, looking at how strange everything was. It was hard to believe it was the same house. On the end table next to the couch, there was a yellow glass vase filled with bright pink fake flowers. And the coffee table didn't have any books on it. Instead there were travel magazines and *Redbook* and a lot of back issues of the Beasley Motivation Seminar newsletter. As I was looking around, I also noticed a photo on the mantel over the fireplace that I'd never seen. Doreen must have put it there last night.

I walked over to it and there encased in a bright pink enamel frame was Josh in his tux and Kimberly Cotton in a sexy red dress! Their Tolo picture, already! (Never having been to a Tolo, I hadn't known that people got the pictures back so fast. I suppose they must have a photographer who does a one-hour developing thing or something. Maybe they take them in the beginning of the dance and then bring them back at the end all developed, but how would I know?

I had to admit, it was a good picture. It was a five-by-seven, very slick like a studio thing, and not a dinky Polaroid.

Well, why not?

Seriously, why not?

Why not just send it?

I mean, who would know?

When I think of things like this I almost expect to hear Bertha Jane's voice, but right then my head was full of schemes of how to pull this off, calculating the time it would take me to get to the copy place to have it copied, then back home to put the photo back on the mantel. In the privacy of my room I could cut Kimberly out of the copy and scan Josh into my computer standing alone in his tux, all ready to E-mail. I was pretty sure it would not be cool to send Allison a picture with another girl in it. Kimberly looked awesome in her dress, too. But maybe it would actually be a good strategy to send the picture of Josh and Kimberly together. Maybe girls like competition, maybe it gets them more interested. I truly have no clue about these things and it makes me wish there was a book called *A Dummy's Guide to Girls*.

I thought about just scanning the photo into my computer, printing it out, and then cutting Kimberly out of the picture, but my printer's not color and photos come out pretty blurry. It might look too cheesy and Allison could get suspicious and wonder why I sent a blurry pic. I looked at my watch; it was ten after four. There should be enough time for me to take the photo to the Copy Mart and get back before any of them got home. One good color copy would be less than a dollar. I checked my wallet: six bucks. I had plenty.

I grabbed the picture off the mantel. "Come on, Fred, we've got business to do." Fred followed me out of the house and jumped in the front seat as I got in the car and checked the gas. Good. A quarter of a tank, more than enough. I started the engine and reached over and rolled the window down part way so he could stick his nose out. Fred likes that a lot.

The Copy Mart is on Madison about fifteen minutes from our house. The traffic in the neighborhood wasn't bad, but once I got on Madison it was pretty slow since it was rush hour. I was frustrated creeping along and worried that I might not get this little project done by the time everyone got home. I even felt like honking, which is not like me because I think it's really dumb to honk when traffic is all stopped up, like that's really going to make it go faster. But I had the urge to honk anyway, just to express myself, I guess. But instead, I turned up the radio and tried to chill.

Two blocks past the light at 23rd and Madison the traffic came to a complete stop. *Great.* Just what we need. I rolled down my window and stuck my head out to see what was going on. About half a block in front of me, I saw a police car and a tow truck. Must be some kind of accident. Just my luck. Of course it was terrible luck for the person who got in a wreck, but I didn't think it was a really bad accident because I hadn't seen an ambulance.

After what seemed like hours, we finally started to move a little, slowly creeping up Madison. Fred had his head stuck out the window just like all the people who stared at the accident as we drove by. Next to the police car, a policewoman was talking to two guys. Both seemed pretty young, maybe my age or early twenties. The tow truck was hooking up an old car that had its fender half off and its rear end dented in. The other car was a new Jeep with its front wheels over the curb and it didn't look messed up at all.

I don't know why, but whenever I see a policeman—or police-woman for that matter—I feel guilty. If one ever comes up to me when I'm in my car, I feel this way even if I don't know what I did. And also it happens even if they've just stopped to have a cup of coffee at McDonald's and they're near me in line; I feel like a criminal or something.

As I inched past the accident, seeing those two guys made me think about this accident I had about six months after I got my license. It was just a fender bender but it was my fault. I had been looking in the rearview mirror, trying to adjust it, and I took my eyes off the road and drove into the car in front of me. I was coming up to a light and only going about five miles an hour, but the lady went nuts even though her fender just got a little scratch, unlike my front fender which fell off. The weird thing was that Dad was okay about it. Not that he was nice exactly, but he didn't have a total meltdown. I've never been sure what kinds of things will set him off. This got me to wondering what he'd do if I didn't make it back in time from the Copy Mart with Josh's Tolo picture and they figured out I'd ripped it off. I realized that in case I got caught, I'd have to think of some reason to tell them why I took it.

The traffic started to pick up and it was four forty-five by the time I parked in front of the Copy Mart. I grabbed the picture, ran in, and got in the line, which actually wasn't that long, but you never know how much time each person will take. Sometimes people have all kinds of complicated stuff they want copied. While I waited I decided to work on my cover story.

Borrowing the photo to take to the school newspaper?

You're not on the school newspaper!

Okay, how 'bout for a school project?

Please. What kind of project? That's so lame.

Okay. Okay. How 'bout for a present?

For who? Kimberly? She just burned your best friend!

For his dad. For Josh's dad. Like a moving-in present.

Maybe.

That's it, dammit. That's the best I can do.

That's the one I went with. I had it copied as a favor to Josh, so he could send one to his dad. It was a moving-in present from me to Josh. I decided to get two copies, one to cut up to send to Allison and one for Josh to send to his dad, in case I needed to use the cover story.

Then it was my turn at the counter. A very pretty Asian girl whose nametag said CAROLINE asked me if she could help me.

"I need two copies of this photo." I put it on the counter, still in the frame.

"Do you want the same size, or reduced or enlarged?"

"Guess I better take it out of the frame first," I mumbled.

"That would help." She smiled.

I turned it over and fumbled with the metal clips that held the back on.

"So what size did you want?"

I slipped it out of the frame. "It's a photo of my stepbrother for a present to send to his dad who lives in Mexico since his mom just married my dad and now they live here with me and my dad, and Fred of course."

Oh my God, why am I saying all this? Like she suspects and I have to explain!

"So you want them the same size?"

"Right, sure. Same size, that'd be fine."

She took the photo and went to the color copy machine. She was very calm. Nothing in her expression showed she knew she was dealing with someone mental. In a few minutes, she was back. I paid for the picture and left, hoping the traffic wouldn't be a mess and I could get back before anyone got home.

Seeing that Asian girl at the Copy Mart made me think of Thao. Not that they looked a lot alike, but just because they were both Asian, I guess. And right about now, Thao was probably having this big relationship with the Nice Guy, with her auntie and everyone in her family happy about it. And what was I doing? This phony weird thing, that's what. I started feeling like a criminal as I drove home, even though I didn't see any police.

It was five-fifteen as I got to our street. I thought I'd pulled it off, since they're usually not home until at least five-thirty. But no such luck. Doreen's car was in the drive. Now what?

I squished the Copy Mart bag under my jacket, got Fred, and went in the house. So far so good. No sign of her in the kitchen.

I peeked around the doorway to the living room. Whew! Empty.

She must be upstairs. I took the photo out of the bag and walked as fast as I could over to the mantel. I stuck it in the frame and put it back where it was and then hotfooted it out of there, but Doreen had put a puny little table with a vase sitting on it next to the couch where we'd never had a table before, and on my way out my foot caught on its leg.

Thud! Crash!

The yellow glass vase hits the deck.

Shards of yellow glass splinter everywhere.

Pink fake flowers are strewn across the living room.

"Jason? Josh? WHO'S THERE!" Doreen comes flying down the stairs.

I run to the kitchen and get the broom and the dustpan.

"Jason! What happened!"

I am back in a flash, madly sweeping up the glass. "Careful, you don't have on shoes," I tell Doreen as if she doesn't know this.

Doreen jumps back, staring at the ground. "My vase! My grandmother's vase. Oh, Jason, what were you doing?"

"Just decided to play catch with it, that's all." I sweep like crazy. Then I look up and her nose is red and I think she is either going to explode or cry.

"I'm sorry."

She bit her lip. "That was in my grandmother's house. She had it when I was a little girl."

"Look, I said I was sorry." I picked up the dustpan and went to the kitchen and put the glass in the trash. When I went back to the living room, she had picked up all the flowers and was gone.

Fine. If you'd kept your grandmother's vase and that stupid table in your condo and not moved in here this never would have happened.

📂 Nine

THE THING WITH THE vase had gotten me in such a bad mood that I didn't feel like sending the picture, so instead of turning on my computer, I just lay around all night and watched the tube. To be honest, I was sorry I broke her vase, I felt bad about it. But it made me mad, too, and I bounced back and forth between feeling guilty and being pissed while I watched a late movie I didn't even care about. It was an old dorky flick with singing and dancing, the kind where the people are talking and then music starts and they jump up and sing. That kind of thing usually makes me laugh, but it ended up getting me more depressed so I finally just shut off the TV and went to bed.

The next morning was Sunday, which was good because I slept late and felt a lot better when I woke up. I got up around noon, relaxed and refreshed and hardly thought about Doreen's vase. I think it's really true that a lot of things seem better in the morning and I jumped out of bed with Allison Gray on my mind, ready to grab the scissors and customize Josh's Tolo picture to meet my personal needs.

It took me a few minutes to find the scissors, but then they surfaced on the floor under a mess of stuff near the spot where I'd cut the shirt to fit Fred. I got the Copy Mart bag and pulled out the photo and held it out in front of me. The scissors were open in my sure and steady hand, poised and ready to slice Josh away from Kimberly.

Then I put the scissors down. The guy really did look like Leonardo, especially in his tux. Allison Gray might get suspicious. Naturally she'd wonder how a guy who looked like that would have time to mess around on the Net when he'd undoubtedly have real girls jumping on him on a daily basis.

Right then and there I decided not to cut it. I would send the whole picture. Kimberly looked sexy and cute, but like a regular girl and not a movie star so the whole thing would be a lot more believable. Allison Gray would think I had a life.

I turned on my computer and scanner. But instead of scanning the picture, I put the photo down and went to the phone, because right then I had a very strong urge to call Thao and remind myself that my entire life wasn't fake, that there was a real girl who knew me. A wonderful, beautiful girl who knew what I looked like and how I sounded and how I acted and she really was in my life even if she was in California and I just had to call her. Of course, Dad would be mad when he saw the phone bill, but I'd just have to deal with it.

Thao's line was busy. I hung up and dialed again a few minutes later.

Still busy. I knew it. She was talking to Nice Guy. They were having long conversations where she lay on her bed with her beautiful dark hair spread over the pillow holding the phone close to her lips, her soft voice saying things to him.

Fine.

Who cares.

I went to my computer, scanned in the photo, put it in a file and signed on AOL. Then I wrote an E-mail to Allison.

> Subject: Jason's pic
> Hi Allison,
> Here's the pic you wanted. It was taken not too long ago at a dance we had. The girl's name is Karen Collins. Sorry I didn't have a recent picture of just me, but since you had this deadline I had to send this one. I know it's cheesy to send a picture with a girl. Hope you don't mind. Looking forward to getting urs!
> Peace,
> Jason

I read it over a bunch of times, then I attached the file with Josh's Tolo picture. Then I imagined Josh Kemple and Kimberly Cotton (alias Jason Kovak and Karen Collins) hurling through cyberspace toward Hawaii in their Tolo clothes, sailing over the Pacific, over the deep blue sea, passing yachts, cruise ships, silver jet planes, satellite signals, and seagulls right into the machine of wonderful Allison Gray. Allison Gray who would send me messages every day from now on, rushing home after school to hang with me in cyberspace. She'd be there in my machine, waiting for me, every day at the same time. Someone I could count on. Someone who would be there. *Allison Gray.* I said her name aloud, and then I hit "Send."

Later that day, Kenny wanted me to go to Tower Records to get some new CDs and cruise around with him for a while. It was fine by me. I didn't like being home on weekends when everyone was there, and it was always great to be with Kenny. But the way it turned out, it would have been a lot better if I'd stayed home and waited to hear from Allison Gray.

We drove around for a while down Broadway on Capitol Hill then over to "the Ave." in the U district, the main drag next to the

University of Washington. Every year it seems to get sleazier and sleazier. We were in the right lane, stopped at the light at University Ave. and 45th. Next to our car, this druggie-looking dude, pasty white, skinny, with stringy brown hair and a ratty beard is practically nodding off against a telephone pole. He's slumped over and then just as the light changes, he falls against our car. This wakes him up and he stares at us with glazed eyes and spits on the car.

"Move your butt, diphead!" Kenny yells.

There is a pickup behind us and the guy starts honking. The druggie falls back against the pole. Kenny flips the bird to the guy behind us and we roar off.

"The Ave's not what it used to be, man," Kenny mumbles. "Let's go to the Village."

I nod and push up my shades, which keep falling down my nose. I am praying that the guy behind us has not gone ballistic and is not about to pull up next to us with a little tantrum of road rage and blow our heads off.

I look back and I see him in his pickup. The window is rolled down and resting on the window is an arm the size of your average redwood tree. I am sure there are tattoos on this arm, obscenities and little sayings like "Mad Dog" and "Kill for Fun."

I push my shades up again and slump down as Kenny drives along, tapping his fingers against the wheel to the song on the radio, an old one by Smashing Pumpkins. Kenny is unconcerned. He is oblivious to the fact that at any moment "Kill for Fun" is going to roar by and obliterate us. I am sure that if this happens it will be punishment for sending Josh's picture to Allison Gray.

The guy pulls out to pass us.

This is it. I duck, hoping the bullets will miss my head.

"Diphead!" The guy yells, then he cuts Kenny off, almost clipping the front left side of the car. Kenny slams on the brakes, my head snaps back, and ahead of us the guy peels down the Ave.

"Let's go to the Village, man." I choke out the words.

Kenny nods. He turns up the radio full blast. He does not chase the guy in the pickup, and I am grateful. Kenny is very aggressive compared to me, but he is not an idiot.

We hang at the Village a long time. It's a fancy mall near the University of Washington. We went in the Gap and checked out the stuff, listened to CDs at Barnes & Noble, then over to QFC where we both got Cokes and some chips. Kenny likes these fancy Tim's potato chips but I like classic chips, just like I like classic Coke. I also got a bag of Oberto beef jerky and a doughnut.

There are tables in a courtyard in the middle of the mall where we sat and ate and watched girls. A lot of girls go to U Village, and they usually seem to congregate where we were sitting, near the Gap. When Kenny looks at girls there is always the distinct possibility that he might start up a conversation and they might talk to him. When I watch the girls, that's what it is: watching. Nothing ever happens. I never get from watching to talking. I suppose that's why I like sending and getting E-mails from Allison Gray. It seems like progress.

It was around six when Kenny dropped me off at my house. I went in the side door and the house smelled funny, it had a strange odor—a weird combination of gardenia perfume and roast chicken. Dad came storming around the corner, which I've noticed is now the typical way he greets me.

"I can't believe you forgot!"

"Forgot what?"

"Jeez, Jason. For once I just wish you'd—"

"It's all right, Jack. We'll just go ahead now," Doreen called from the dining room.

"Wash up and come in the dining room," Dad ordered.

I went in the bathroom and while I was washing my hands, it came back to me. Doreen had said she wanted us to have Sunday dinner and she made a little speech about it. She said she recognized that our schedules were different with everyone coming and going at different times, but that it was important to have at least one meal together every week. This dinner was supposed to take place all sitting around the table together and not in front of the TV. We were going to have Sunday dinner every week, like a family.

I went in the dining room and sat across from Josh. Dad and Doreen were on either end of the table and there was a big roast chicken in front of Dad. Also there was gravy and mashed potatoes, stuff I'd love to eat if I wasn't full of chips, a doughnut and Oberto beef jerky. When they passed the food to me, even though I wasn't hungry, I took a little to be polite, because I did feel bad about forgetting. I really hadn't blown it off on purpose.

Dad is telling Josh stuff about Kovak Kans. "The important thing, Josh, is to check the sites every day. We need to maintain the equipment, not just deliver it."

"Does it matter when you check?" Josh asks.

"Better midday, if possible. So if there are any problems you can see to it before the crew gets off at the end of the day."

As I am picking at the little plop of mashed potatoes I hear a noise, like crying, somewhere. My fork freezes in midair. I listen, and I hear it again.

"Where's Fred?"

"In the basement," Dad says as he chews his chicken.

"He's stuck down there!" I jump up and Dad sticks his arm out and grabs me.

"Hold on a minute. Fred's fine. Doreen doesn't think it's polite to have an animal around while we're eating. You can let him out when we're done."

"Where'd you put him?"

"He's in the closet at the bottom of the stairs."

The crying got louder. It was high and mournful and it ripped my heart out. I looked at these people sitting around the dining-room table having their family Sunday dinner in my house and I wanted to dump mashed potatoes on their heads.

Fred's cries became louder and more desperate as he heard me coming down the basement stairs. Then there was a thud, followed by another and another as he jumped and threw himself against the door.

"JASON!"

Dad is at the top of the stairs, yelling. I open the closet and Fred leaps out, panting like crazy. The closet stinks. He has peed in it. Fine. Too bad he didn't dump in there as well, a nice mound of dog turds on Dad's golf clubs.

Fred licks me all over my face, practically knocking me over. He jumps in my arms and I carry him up the stairs.

Dad puts his hand out to stop me.

"Don't even think about it." I stare at him and push past his hand.

He's quiet for a second. But I hear him yelling again as I carry Fred to the car. He's still yelling as I back the car out of the drive. Fred sticks his nose out the window, he keeps panting and he's still kind of frantic. I drive down the street, and I don't look back.

I don't know how long I drove around the neighborhood. I didn't have anywhere to go so I just kept driving. Every once in a while I'd stop somewhere and hug Fred, then I'd drive around some more. One of the first places I stopped was across from my old school, John Muir Elementary. I had a kindergarten teacher there who liked me. Ms. Aoki, I'll never forget her. She got me some special left-handed scissors and helped me cut things out of colored paper. When I made something she never asked me what it was, she just said it was very nice. She made origami for us, cranes and birds out of white paper. In first grade, I was in something they called a first-second split. We had two teachers, Ms. Maynard and Ms. Tracy, and they sang and played instruments. I loved them, too. I always liked to play the tambourine in that class.

For a second I thought about going to Kenny's house. I even started to drive in that direction, but when I got to his street I kept going because I knew deep down Kenny wouldn't really understand about Fred. Mrs. Newman is allergic and they've never had pets. Not that he wouldn't try because I knew he would, but the last thing I'd be able to do right now was explain anything to anybody. It was too much, I just couldn't do it and I'd rather be alone.

I drove down Rainier heading south. It always gets me how within just a few miles people live so differently. There are big houses all along Lake Washington and then small ones and public housing between Rainier and Martin Luther King Way. It never seemed fair to me how some people get to be born into families that live in big houses near Lake Washington and other people are born into families that live in public housing. This also bothered Bertha Jane and it was the kind of thing she talked about when she ran for mayor. She used to say that there were mostly two kinds of people in the USA: people who thought that if you were poor it was your own fault and people who when they saw a poor person thought, There, but by the Grace of God, go I. Bertha Jane wasn't someone who went around talking about God, just every once in awhile the name would pop up in her conversation. I know she went to church, though, because her church sponsored people from Vietnam and that's how she met Thao.

I drove down to Rainier Beach and then turned back by South Shore Middle School. South Shore was close to Lake Washington and I thought it was a cool place to have a school, right next to the lake like that. But probably if I'd gone there I would have had a hard time staying in class; it would have been more fun to feed the ducks. Which is what I felt like doing just then, except that I didn't have any bread. Even if I did, Fred would want to get out of the car with me, then he'd chase them and it would not be a good experience for the ducks or me. One of the things I always liked about ducks was that the mother and father ducks stay together, for life I think. At least that's what someone told me once.

I guess I was making a loop, because from South Shore Middle School I headed back, going north again along the lake. Fred was still panting so I switched the radio station to King Classic FM. Maybe some nice classical music would help him forget that he'd been locked up.

The lake was calm, almost like glass, and I decided to drive into Seward Park and take Fred for a walk. He'd probably like to swim, too, to take his mind off things. I turned into the lot and parked next to the Seward Park Art Studio where they have pottery classes. One time Mom signed me up for a kids' class there and I made some stuff, little bowls and a bird sculpture. I actually still have the bird thing, it was a nest with little pottery eggs in it, and the bird was separate so you could take it off the nest and see the little eggs in there. I think I was in about the third grade. Mom arranged for a high-school girl to drive me there after school, but I forget her name.

Fred was thrilled to get out of the car, and he tore across the parking lot, making a beeline for the lake. You get fined if you don't have your dog on a leash, but it was close to seven and even though there were people in the park, I was sure by now the Dog Gestapo would probably be off duty. That's what I call the animal control, the way they hunt down innocent dogs whose only crime is not being on a leash. I can understand if they need to take in a mean dog that could hurt people, but the only kind I've ever seen them arrest is someone's friendly dog that got out of the yard by mistake, the kind that's easy to stuff in their truck.

I found a nice stick by the side of the path, whistled for Fred, and went down the bank to the water. Fred was leaping around the stick like crazy, jumping for joy. He has really recovered from his ordeal, I thought, as I flung the stick out into the lake. Fred tore after it, ducked his head under the water a little as he got it in his mouth then turned, lifting his head up as he paddled back to shore. Fred trotted over to me and dropped the stick, eager to do it again. I think Fred could chase sticks all day, he loves it so much. Seriously, I don't think he'd quit until he dropped. Fred really needs me to look out for him when it comes to things like this or he'd overdo it and collapse. I am Fred's designated driver in many areas of his life.

As I watched Fred with the stick in his mouth, I remembered something Bertha Jane told me about dogs, right before she died. She said that the Abenaki Indians believed that when you die and it is time to cross over into the spirit world, all the dogs you ever had in your life hold on to a log with their teeth and it is on this log that you must walk in order to get to the spirit world. Bertha

Jane loved animals, especially dogs, and I'm sure that in her life she was so good to all the dogs she owned that they would hold that log with all their heart to make it steady for her.

I went to a point at the north end of the park where there's a rocky beach and threw the stick for Fred a few more times. Across from the beach, there's a bench in front of the woods where I like to sit and look out at the lake. Fred seemed to be slowing down so I called him and went over there. I sat on the bench, patting Fred's wet head, and imagined telling Dad if he wasn't nice to Fred that when it was time to cross over to the spirit world, Fred might not hold the stick too well. If he locked him in the closet again, Fred might just let that stick drop and who could blame him? (Of course, telling Dad this would only confirm to him that I am nuts.)

I sat there patting Fred and watched the people going by on bikes and roller skates and with dogs on leashes mostly. I like watching people, wondering where they live and what kind of lives they have. Where would they all go tomorrow, Monday morning? To a job? Or school? What did they do when they weren't here roller-blading around the park? *And what would I do tomorrow?*

And from now on?

I didn't want to live in my car with Fred and I didn't have money for dog food (or people food for that matter). My birthday and Christmas money was about tapped. There was only one way I could get out of there and I knew it.

I had to get a job.

I decided right then I'd have to look immediately, leave the park this second, and hit all the fast-food places on Rainier. I jumped up from the bench. I think Fred was disappointed that I didn't go back to the beach, but I knew I needed to start looking—it was urgent. When they locked Fred in the closet, they didn't know it, but a line had been drawn in the sand. I wasn't going back there for any longer than I had to and the only way out was to make some money.

But there was a little delay before we could leave the parking lot. A couple in front of us was getting a stroller out of their car. They had to lift the stroller out of the trunk and set it up, then get their little baby out of its car seat and get it strapped in the stroller. Fred and I had to sit in the car and wait until they were out of the way, so I just patted him and watched while they did all this stuff.

You know what, little baby? You have a great life. All you have to do is eat and sleep and say goo and stuff like that, and these people take you to the park and you can just sit there while they push you around. You have a great life and you don't even know it.

As soon as the people with the stroller were out of the way, I started the car and we left the park. I drove west until I got to Wilson and headed back south. A bunch of streets along here have dead ends and I wasn't sure which ones would go all the way through to Rainier, so I just picked a street and took my chances. *Pick a street, any street.* And this is what was really weird. I just picked one without even thinking, but as I drove along this street (I hadn't even bothered to check out the name of it) I had this feeling that I was meant to be on this exact street. It had ordinary houses, nothing unusual, but in the middle of the block on the right-hand side there was a church. I saw it up ahead and I knew I'd been there, only once before, but I'd been there. It was Bertha Jane's church.

It was almost eight and it was starting to get dark. I slowed down in front of the church and I noticed a lady on her hands and knees by the flower bed next to the front door. She happened to look up as I was inching by and she smiled. When I saw her face, I pulled closer to the curb and stopped the car. Still smiling, she stood up, wiped her hands on her jeans, and came over to the car.

"Can I help you?"

"I don't know."

"This is Fletcher, 4366 Fletcher Street."

"Did you know Bertha Jane Fillmore?"

She paused and bent down toward the car. "Yes. She was my dear friend."

"Mine, too." ' Then I lost it, and I had to turn away, pretending to see something across the street.

"Would you like to come in?" She motioned toward the church.

"I can't leave my dog."

"Your dog can come."

"In there?"

"Why not? All creatures great and small."

Fred and I got out of the car and followed her inside. I wasn't sure why I did this except that there was something about her that seemed like Bertha Jane, although it wasn't her looks, because there wasn't much of a resemblance. Bertha Jane was small with white hair that fell in wisps across her face. I don't know if she had always been small or maybe she was so little because of the cancer, but this woman was almost as tall as I was and she had thick, curly red hair. She seemed strong and healthy and much younger than Bertha Jane, although it's hard to tell ages. Bertha Jane was eighty-three when I met her; my dad and mom are in their early forties, and I guessed this woman was somewhere inbetween.

Starting to cry like that had snuck up on me. It's been like that ever since Bertha Jane died. It comes out of nowhere and I never know what will set it off. Sadness just wells up inside me like a sudden storm that comes with no warning, and my eyes fill with tears as if some button had been pushed.

We went inside the church and I stopped to look at a sign on a stand in the middle of the large hallway, trying to focus my attention so I wouldn't fall apart again. The sign was black with little stick-on white letters, the kind that could be changed around.

Sunday

  11:00 A.M. Fletcher St. Congregational Church

  2:00 P.M. Samoan Christian Church

  5:00 P.M. Columbia City Unitarian Universalist Congregation

Friday

  7:00 P.M. Temple Emmanuel

"We have three churches and one synagogue that meet here." She pointed to the sign. "Fletcher Street owns the building, and the Samoans, the Unitarians, and the Jewish congregation are renters." She held out her hand to let Fred sniff. "What's his name?"

"Fred."

"Looks like he's been for a swim."

"He's still pretty wet. Maybe we better leave."

"Wait here a minute." She crossed the hall and went around a corner and came back with some paper towels. "We're running low on these. In fact I've got to remember to put it on the list to get more at Costco for the dispensers." She handed me some of the towels, and I wiped his paws while she wiped his head and his back.

"Good dog." She patted Fred's head when she was done. "That should do it. Now he can take the tour, if you'd like to look around. There's a lot of Bertha Jane in this place."

She walked across the big hall to three sets of doors and took some keys out of her pocket.

"Are you sure your boss won't mind?"

"My boss?"

"If Fred and I go in there—"

"I think it's all right. I'm the minister." Then she cracked up and I felt like an idiot. "Look, I'm sorry, it just hit me that you thought I was the janitor."

"Well, you were working in the flower bed, and then you said that stuff about getting paper towels—"

"Please, I didn't mean to laugh at you. It just struck me as funny, that's all. Besides, I never introduced myself." She wiped her hand on her jeans and held it out. "I'm Susie Burns. Everyone calls me Susie or Reverend Susie."

"I'm Jason Kovak," I said as we shook hands.

"I thought you might be. Bertha Jane stopped coming to church about the time you went to work for her. She wanted to save her strength for her campaign for mayor. We were pretty worried about her, but she told us not to, because she'd hired you."

She unlocked the door and inside was a regular church with pews and a pulpit in the front. I was surprised when I looked in there. Maybe because she didn't look anything like the way I thought a minister would look, I didn't expect the church to look like a church. It wasn't too big; it might seat a hundred people if they were all squished together. I followed her in and I couldn't believe my dog and I were standing in a church with this minister in her jeans. It was very weird.

"This is the sanctuary. See the curtains in the back?" She pointed to green curtains on either side of a cross. "They were Bertha Jane's idea. They stay open like they are now for the Christian congregations and then close in front of the cross for Temple Emmanuel's service and for ours. They put the Torah on the altar in front of the curtains and we have a chalice we light. Bertha Jane thought it would be ridiculous to try to raise a bunch of money to put up our own building when there was a perfectly good building right here that people could share."

She led us out of the sanctuary and down the hall and pointed to some stairs. "That goes down to the basement. We have a potluck there every Sunday after the service. Bertha Jane usually brought tuna fish casserole and it was a hit with everyone except the vegetarians." She pulled out her keys again in front of a door at the end of the hall. "This is the office. I'll show you the plaque we have in her memory."

The room was large with a desk and a computer, file cabinets and library tables against the walls filled with papers. There was an old rug in the middle of the room and a lot of beat-up couches and furniture around it, sort of like a living room.

She pointed to photos on the wall. "Here's Bertha Jane and these are the charter members of our congregation." Under the picture of Bertha Jane there was a wooden plaque. Her name and the lettering under it looked like it had been carved by hand.

And I'll bring you hope when hope is hard to find
And I'll bring a song of love and a rose in wintertime.

"That's from her favorite song," she explained. "I suppose you know how she loved her garden."

"I stopped there on my way to the hospital to bring her one."

"A rose?"

"Yeah. I thought they'd probably all be dead, since it was November, but there was one left."

"Waiting for you, I suppose."

That seemed like a weird thing to say, but I tried not to show it.

"Bertha Jane would have thought the meeting we had about her memorial was hilarious. Once she said she thought sometimes people in our denomination were like dogs barking at each other at the park, each one needed to have its say on everything. And the meeting was exactly like that—no one could agree on one memorial so we finally ended up having a bunch of different things. There's a tile with her name on it in the floor at the Pike Place Market, and benches with her nameplate attached at a number of parks, and the Bertha Jane Fillmore Scholarship for a Columbia City student to attend college. I think that's the one she would have liked the best, she liked kids so much."

"Did you know Thao?"

"Sure. I was there when she first came, the day she met Bertha Jane."

"She's in California now."

"I know, some of us helped her move to her aunt's after Bertha Jane died."

"I call her once in a while. Sometimes we talk about Bertha Jane."

"Everyone misses her."

I felt like saying I hate that she died, but I just nodded.

"So where are you working now, Jason?"

"Nowhere, but I'm job hunting. In fact—"

"I can't believe this."

"What?"

Reverend Susie shook her head and smiled. "Serendipity, I guess." She looked out the window. "But it makes you wonder."

"Wonder what?" I thought this woman was kind of strange. Not that she wasn't nice, but maybe just a little bit off.

"I've been in a real bind because Carla Cruz, my assistant, got a full scholarship to the U and had to quit her job here." She paused and smiled. "She does everything from taking out the garbage to folding the newsletter and working on the computer. The job's yours if you want it." She said this without batting an eye while she patted Fred.

My heart sped up. What was happening here? Why had it happened that her assistant had just quit? Why did I start looking for a job today? Was Bertha Jane setting this up? Or was it just some kind of coincidence? Why did I drive down this street? I kept my head down, patting Fred, almost afraid to breathe. "I can start right now."

"That's incredible. Well, this was just meant to be, that's all."

"I can come every day after school, or evenings and weekends— whatever you want."

Reverend Susie let out a big sigh. "How 'bout starting after school tomorrow? Could you be here at four?"

"Sure."

"You can bring Fred if you want," she said casually.

This was getting crazy. I stared at the floor again.

"I mean, only if you want to."

I had to look away for a minute before I could answer. Finally I said, "I think Fred would like that very much."

As I left I knew I would never be able to explain or understand why I picked that street, and how it was that Reverend Susie Burns was out in the yard at that exact moment, and that her assistant had just quit so that she needed to hire someone just as I was heading out to find a job. But it had the feeling of something that was planned. I'll never know if that's true, but whatever the cause of all those events coinciding, I was grateful that I'd been in the right place at the right time. And I also knew that I wouldn't have to spend the night in the car with Fred, I could go home. I don't know how it worked, but Reverend Susie (even though she was a little weird) had given me some kind of protection from them, like an invisible suit of armor and I could go back and face whatever garbage was there.

But in spite of the armor, I still felt relieved when I saw that the house was dark and that they'd all gone out somewhere. It was quiet and Fred and I slipped in and went down to my room. Fred jumped on my bed and I was going to lie down with him and listen to my Discman for a while, but I decided to just check my E-mail first. I'd gotten into the habit of checking it automatically whenever I got home.

I turned on my computer and typed in my password on AOL. In a minute the little yellow envelope popped up and the guy said, "You've got mail." Probably more junk E-mail I thought as I opened it: sex, get-rich-quick schemes, find a dentist, all the usual crap.

But it wasn't. It was from Surfsup10!

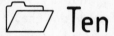 **Ten**

I SAT ON MY BED staring at Allison Gray's picture. It had come with her E-mail just like she promised. She was so cute, I wondered for a minute if she had done what I had (sent someone else's picture), although what she wrote made me think that it really was a picture of her. I had printed it out so I wouldn't have to turn on my computer and go on-line every time I wanted to read it.

subject: ur pics

Hi Jason,
Well here i am, i almost didn't send it after i got urs! u didn't tell me u looked like that! i didn't mind that it was a picture of u and ur date. After all i was the 1 who said to send it or u'd b history. i don't exactly look like my pic. i wear glasses. i'm allergic to contacts but when i'm 20 i'm having laser surgery that's supposed to fix it so i'm not nearsighted. They do it in Europe all the time but it's newer here. i have

to wait until i'm 20 because they want to make sure my eyes are stable, whatever that means. i'm sure this is totally boring reading about my eyes, but i just wanted u to know that i always take my glasses off for pictures. This was taken at a beach a few miles from my house. Send me an IM soon k? i'll be on-line probably by eight tomorrow.
Later,
Allison

I looked at her picture again; even with glasses she'd be cute but she wasn't blond like I thought. Her hair looked more dark brown, not shiny black like Thao's, but just kind of brown. It came to about her shoulders and it was straight and sort of fluffed out a little. I couldn't tell how tall she was—she was leaning back against a palm tree. But as I studied the picture, I noticed a park trash can near the tree and when I compared her height to the can, it didn't seem that she was especially tall or short, just sort of average, I'd say. She was wearing khaki shorts and a blue-and-white striped T-shirt, and she had a nice tan. She looked like an outdoor person, healthy and athletic, not like a girl who had long red nails and stayed in her bedroom all day putting on makeup.

From the moment it arrived, I looked at Allison's picture every chance I had. I even got up in the middle of the night to look at it. And this morning, here I was staring at her again. I woke up early so I could leave for school without seeing any of them (Dad, Doreen, and Josh). That's how I thought of these people now: *Them.*

As I showered, it dawned on me that it had been easy to get up early. It's funny how sometimes when there's a change, you don't always recognize it right away. After Bertha Jane died, jumping out of bed in the morning was as hard as parachuting from a plane would be for me with my fear of heights. Getting up was just that awful. The alarm would go off and I would be sick with dread. But today, not only had I gotten out of bed pretty easily, but I'd even set my alarm so I could get up early. Amazing! The other weird thing I noticed was that everything actually seemed brighter and I'm not talking about my mood. I mean, it was as if there was really more light, like a dimmer switch had been moved ever so slightly and things just got lighter.

I left the house before anyone was up and went to McDonald's. I usually don't eat much for breakfast, just grab a bagel or a banana. But today there was so much time to kill, I had two sausage biscuits with eggs. I took my tray to an empty table where someone had left a newspaper and read the comics while I ate. The food was pretty good and as I looked around at the other people getting their coffee and eating, I decided this could be an okay life. McDonald's was a friendlier place than my house, and if things got worse at home, maybe Fred and I could live in Reverend Susie's church. I could work in exchange for the rent, and with any money I earned I could eat at McDonald's and get food for Fred. After I finished eating, I folded up the paper and left it for the next person. It was incredible how great it was not to feel trapped.

And at school, there was something fun about going to class with a picture of a cute girl from Hawaii in my pocket. I sort of felt like a different guy. In homeroom when Sarah Klein came in and sat next to me, I even started up a little conversation! The same thing happened with Nina Brim and Jennifer Sider in my geometry class. (Of course it's not like I turned into Kenny—that guy is fearless when it comes to girls.) This was about being able to talk to someone I already knew and I just wasn't as uptight because I had Allison Gray right there in my wallet.

After school, I went straight to work. Even though Reverend Susie said I could bring Fred, I was afraid if I went home for him I might be late and the last thing I wanted to do was mess up this job. I got there right at four and she was in the yard again when I pulled up.

"Hi, Jason." She stood up and wiped her hands on her jeans. "Where's Fred?"

"I was afraid if I went home I might be late."

"It's okay to start at four-fifteen if you want to pick him up." She walked toward the door. "Come on in."

"The flowers look nice." I glanced at the bed where she had been working as I followed her into the church.

"Thanks. Flowers are a necessity to me. Somebody said, 'Find a way to make beauty necessary, find a way to make necessity beautiful.' I've got a head full of quotes, but half the time I can't remember who said them, so they're all attributed to 'somebody.'"

In the office Reverend Susie motioned for me to sit down. "Actually, sometimes forgetting things scares me, but I'm not sure what I can do about it except laugh and make a lot of lists."

"Bertha Jane used to have a joke, sort of a little saying when she forgot things."

"She did, that's right. Do you remember how it went?"

"No."

"Me either." Reverend Susie laughed. She sat at her desk and started rummaging through some papers. "The problem is, I forget where I put the lists." Then phone rang. "Just a second, I'll have to get this," she said as she picked it up and answered, "Columbia City Unitarian Universalist Congregation."

There was a long pause and I thought I should probably leave so she could talk privately, so I stood up to go out in the hall, but she motioned for me to stay. I sat back down and waited. While she was on the phone she didn't say much; she just nodded and said "uh-huh" a lot. Then she started frantically rummaging through her desk, looking for something.

"It's not part of the pastoral counseling here, but there's a really good resource for you that I can recommend. Sure. If you hang on a minute, I'll get the number." She put the phone down and looked in her desk some more, then she picked up the phone again. "I'm sorry, I seem to have misplaced the number, I'll have to call you back." She grabbed a pen and wrote down the person's number. "Sure, okay. I'll call you right back." Reverend Susie hung up. "I have that number in my book, which has got to either be in my bag or my briefcase."

She looked in her briefcase for a few minutes. "Nope, must be in my bag." Reverend Susie went to the table next to the window where a large woven bag lay on a pile of books. "They want marriage counseling and I always refer people to the Family Counseling Center for that." She smiled as she pulled an address book out of her bag and leafed through it. "I'm divorced and I've found it doesn't inspire credibility when people want marriage counseling."

I laughed although I wasn't sure if she meant this to be a joke because I really didn't quite know how to take her. I waited some more while she called the person back, figuring that she'd tell me what work she wanted me to do as soon as she got off the phone. The call only took a few minutes and when she hung up, she looked over at me but instead of talking about the work, asked if I wanted some tea.

"Tea? I keep the water heated on the hot plate." She went over to it and fixed herself a cup. "Sure you don't want some?"

"No thanks."

"I like tea with honey, but I'm always running out." She squeezed a clear plastic bear over her cup. "Guess this little guy's about done."

"I can go to the store if you want."

Susie sat across from me on the couch. "Thanks, but it's not really a priority. Right now the priority is how you're doing."

"How I'm doing what?" I was becoming very convinced that Reverend Susie was a little out there, and I was also starting to worry. Maybe I hadn't really understood this deal, maybe she wasn't going to pay me and she thought I was going to do volunteer work or something.

"My sermon's going to be about how process is more important than product. That's one of those phrases I don't know if I read somewhere or if I made it up, I think I might have made it up, though, because we have so many technology companies around that are killing their people so they can beat the next guy. It's kind of a spin on the journey being more important than the destination."

"Oh."

"Do you see what I mean?"

"Not really, I guess."

"It's just that the process of people connecting with each other is more important that the thing they end up with. If you did a job, say, fixed the door handle on the Sunday school room, but you and I never felt any human connection, or worse, if I was abrupt or abrasive toward you in my hurry to get it fixed, I would have valued the lesser thing. I would have valued the product, the fixed handle, over you and our ability to connect as human beings."

"Does the door handle need fixing?"

"That was just hypothetical."

"What exactly do you want me—"

"Of course, there are exceptions, I admit. Life-threatening emergencies, something of that nature." She grabbed a pencil and scribbled some notes. "Like if the house caught on fire nothing would be more important than getting the people out even if you had to scream at them. But then, that's valuing the people more than anything so maybe it isn't so different." She scribbled some more, then looked up. "You look confused—"

"I was wondering if you thought I was a volunteer?"

Reverend Susie put her pencil down. "I didn't mention the pay?"

"Not exactly."

"I'm sorry, Jason. Bertha Jane thought so much of you and I was so excited that you were available that I must have forgotten to mention it."

"It's okay."

"It's six dollars an hour."

"Really? Great. So what should I do today?"

She looked at her watch. "I guess we better get to the basement and start painting."

"So that's what you want done first, painting the basement?"

"No, painting scenery for a short play that will be part of the service." She took a sip of her tea and then quickly put her cup down. "Oh, I didn't think about your clothes."

I looked down at what I was wearing.

"How 'bout if you went home and got into old clothes, something you wouldn't mind painting in."

"Sure."

"We can talk while we work. I still want to know how you are, I got off the track thinking about my sermon."

"Okay. I'll be back in about ten minutes."

"Take your time, and get Fred if you want. I've got to make some calls and bring in the stuff from the flower bed."

I looked at my watch as I went out to the car, hopefully it was still early enough so when I got home I wouldn't run into *Them*. Or if someone was home, maybe I could dash in and out so fast that I'd escape any kind of encounter. I was not up for an encounter with alien forces, but unfortunately, as I turned onto our street, I saw Dad's car in the drive.

I sat in my car for a minute with the motor running, debating whether or not to just turn around and go back to work. Who cares about clothes? I could be careful and if I did get some paint on my stuff, so what? But then I imagined Fred getting locked in the closet while they ate dinner and I knew I had to go in for him, just the way a guy goes behind enemy lines to rescue his buddy. So I went in, poised for the rescue. Charging the house with my head down, I tore right into the kitchen. Right into an ambush. The second I pushed the door open, Dad was in my face.

"Jason, I came home early so you couldn't weasel out of talking to me. Sit down." He clenched his teeth and pointed to the kitchen table.

"I can't."

"What do you mean you can't?"

"I have to change my clothes, get Fred, and get back to work."

"Fine. Now I've heard everything." He was standing there glaring at me when we heard the door unlock and Josh came in. He mumbled "hi," then disappeared like a phantom.

"I am sick and tired of your damn lies." Dad slammed the table with his fist.

"It's not a lie!"

"You expect me to believe that you've got a job where you can take that damn dog!"

"He's not a damn dog!"

We heard Josh's door slam so hard it sounded like something had exploded.

"What the hell's wrong with you, Jason?" Dad started pacing around.

"What's wrong with you! Just once in my life I wish you'd stand up for *me*. She comes in here and gets rid of all our stuff, takes over everything, locks Fred up, and you never once, *not once* ever asked me about how I felt about any of it. You never listen to me!"

"You're the one that doesn't listen! I tell you to be here for dinner and you forget. You forget every damn thing I tell you!

"Tell is right—you're always telling me what to do!"

Then there are footsteps running down the stairs and Josh stands in the doorway. "I've got a test tomorrow—I wish you'd just shut up!"

"Fine by me. I'm outta here. Come on, Fred." I grabbed Fred and tore out of the house. I jumped in my car in such a hurry I didn't even open the window so Fred could stick his nose out. I jammed the gears in reverse and peeled out of the driveway. Dad ran after me and stood in the drive yelling something, but I couldn't hear it.

Maybe Reverend Susie would let me sleep at the church tonight. I would do this outstanding job at the painting or anything else she wanted me to do and then I could approach her about it. That couch in her office would probably be fine to sleep on and I think there was a refrigerator in the building. Maybe there'd be some leftover food in there, or I could hide in the bushes next to our garage and scope out our house until I was sure they were gone, then sneak in and get a stash of food to last until my first paycheck.

When we got to the church Reverend Susie met us at the door. Fred jumped out of the car and ran over to her with his tail whirling like an airplane propeller.

"Couldn't find any old clothes?" She patted Fred, who was busy licking her hand.

"My dad was there. He didn't believe I have a job and we had a fight—so I left."

"Do you want me to tell him? I'd be happy to call, if you think that would help."

"He's hopeless, besides I don't mind if I get paint on my clothes."

"We've probably got some old thing around here you can put on. I'll just have to think where, that's all."

"I can paint like this, really."

"I'm pretty sure there's an old shirt in the closet in the office. Let's just take a quick look."

I followed her to the office and waited with Fred while she looked in the closet. She was on her hands and knees, going through a box on the floor. "I gather you didn't want to see him."

"My dad?"

"Yeah." She pulled more stuff out of the box.

"He's always yelling at me. All he does is tell me what to do. He never wants to know what I think about anything. I don't think he even knows me, and I don't know how he could. He never listens to me."

"Here, this should work." She stood up and kicked the box back in the closet and held out a faded denim shirt. I took it and put it on while she went over to a file cabinet.

"Did Bertha Jane ever show you the Listening poem?" She opened the file cabinet and leafed through some folders. "I'd be a lot more with-it if I kept this on the computer and just printed it out when I wanted a copy." She flipped through more folders and then stopped and pulled one out of the cabinet. "Here it is." She handed it to me. "Ever see this?"

I glanced at it and I knew what it was right away. "Sure. Bertha Jane kept it in her cane." I smiled, remembering how surprised I was when Bertha Jane first unscrewed the top of her cane, a weird cane that was hollow inside where she kept special papers and things like this poem. But I couldn't remember what had happened to the copy she gave me.

LISTENING

When I ask you to listen to me and you change the subject, I feel I am alone.

When I ask you to listen to me and you start giving advice, you have not done what I have asked.

When I ask you to listen to me and you begin to tell me why I shouldn't feel that way, you are trampling on my feelings.

When I ask you to listen to me and you feel you have to do something to solve my problem, you have failed me, strange as it may seem.

Listen! All I asked was that you listen, not talk or do—just hear me.

Advice is cheap: twenty-five cents will get you both Dear Abby and Billy Graham in the same newspaper.

All I can I do for myself. I am not helpless. Maybe discouraged and faltering but not helpless.

When you do something for me that I can and need to do for myself, you contribute to my fear and inadequacy.

But, when you accept the simple fact that I feel what I feel, no matter how distressful, then I can get about the business of understanding what's behind the feeling.

Now, more than ever I need to talk.

And I will listen to you. It will go much better for us.

We will be closer.

—Anonymous cancer patient

"Could I keep this? Bertha Jane gave me a copy once, but I don't know where it is."

"Sure."

I folded the poem and stuck it in my pocket and then followed Reverend Susie down to the basement. As Fred and I went down the stairs behind her, this strange thing happened that I didn't plan at all. I began telling her all kinds of stuff and it was like I'd popped my cork and everything (except the stuff about Allison Gray) fizzed and bubbled over. I told her about Thao leaving, about hardly ever talking to my mom, about my dad, Doreen, Josh, and especially about Fred getting locked in the basement.

"The thing is, I hate fighting with him. I even showed that poem to my dad right after Bertha Jane died and for a while it seemed like he was trying. But lately, if he acts like I even exist, it's just to yell at me. His big thing is that I'm unmotivated. He also thinks I'm nuts."

"Grief can make you feel nuts. Grab that, will you?" Reverend Susie pointed to the end of a large sheet of butcher paper, then she tossed me a roll of masking tape. "We'll tape it up to the wall here."

"Like this?" I held my side of the paper against the wall at my shoulder height.

"Little higher, I think." She looked over as I moved it up. "That's good. Toss me the tape when you get yours up there."

"Okay."

I tossed her the tape back. "Hold this a second, okay?" She handed me her part of the paper and I held it up while she tore off some pieces of tape. "And there's nothing more unmotivating."

"What's unmotivating?"

"Grief. You can't budge it. It really flattens you, makes you mad, too." She went in the kitchen and came back with some brushes and two jars of poster paint and brought them over to me. "The scenery is supposed to be water, blue waves with maybe a little white for foam or whitecaps."

"I'll put the blue on first. Should I cover the whole thing blue?"

"Sure."

I started painting while she rolled up the rest of the butcher paper and put stuff away in the kitchen.

"I'm not saying he's a monster. He never hits me or anything. It's just that he doesn't like me or think there's much good about me."

"Sometimes that hurts as much as being hit," she called from the kitchen. After a few minutes she came out carrying a big plate. "I wish I knew who this belonged to, sometimes we get all our stuff mixed up with Temple Emmanuel's." She stopped and looked at what I'd been painting. "That looks great."

"Could Fred and I sleep here tonight?" I hadn't planned on asking her so soon, but it popped out.

"Is it that bad at home?"

I didn't say anything. He didn't hit me. *How bad is bad?*

"If you didn't go home, wouldn't your father worry? Maybe even call the police."

"Could you get in trouble?"

"Possibly."

"I wouldn't want that."

"Jason, I can't tell you what to do. But I have a pretty good idea of what Bertha Jane and Thao meant to you and I'm glad you're here. It's a place you can come to in your mind even when you're physically at home or at school or anywhere, if you get what I mean."

If Reverend Susie was suggesting I have an out-of-body experience and fly off to her church in my mind, I thought she was getting out there again. I didn't want to just travel there in my mind, I wanted my body to come along, too. But I didn't push it, because her attitude about everything was so different from my dad's that I felt like a starving person getting food for the first time in a long time. And when that happens, you don't care if the cook might be a little off.

 Eleven

D AD POUNCED ON ME AGAIN the minute I got home from work. Same old, same old. He must have just been sitting around waiting to hear the sound of my car in the drive.

"Where the hell have you been, Jason?"

"I told you, at work."

Dad started to yell, but then he stopped himself, actually looking at me for a change. "You've got paint all over your clothes."

"They're not my clothes. My boss gave them to me to wear while I painted."

"And just who is this boss, may I ask?"

"Reverend Susie."

"Reverend who?"

"Susie. Susie Burns, she's a minister."

"What?" He looked as shocked as if I'd said she was a prostitute.

"A minister, of a church, only it's not called a church. They call it a congregation."

"Now I've heard everything. Exactly what church is this, Jason?"

"The Columbia City Unitarian Universalist Congregation."

Dad looked suspicious. "And this is a real thing. I mean, you're going to get paid and everything? For painting the place, or what?"

"I get paid. I was painting trees and the ocean."

Dad gave me that look again, like I was mental. "Spare me the details, Jason. But now that you have a job, if this Susie person really is going to pay you, all I can say is you better start paying off your phone bill." Then he left and I heard him go in the den and turn on the TV.

Great, Jason. I'm really proud of you. Way to go! I knew you could do it! What kind of job is it? How'd you get it? Tell me all about it, I'm really interested.

There was only one person in my life who would understand about Reverend Susie, and I went down to my room to call Thao, hoping more than anything that she'd be home. While the phone was ringing, I took the Listening poem out of my pocket and read it again, wishing there was some way I could reprogram my dad's brain with this poem. Some way I could just put it in there, like transferring a file into a computer.

"Thao?"

"Jason. Great! How are you?"

Thao sounded so happy to hear from me, I felt like the sun had come out and turned everything bright.

"I met someone you know and I got a job there. Reverend Susie."

"Reverend Susie Burns? Sure, I know her. She helped us when we first came. She is friend of Bertha Jane."

"I know. She's great."

"Yes. Really great person. My auntie knows her, too."

"I thought about you today a lot, Thao."

"Really?"

"She gave me this poem about listening. It was one Bertha Jane had, she kept it in her cane."

"I remember that. It was very good."

Then I told Thao about how I just happened to turn down the street by the church and Reverend Susie was right there in the yard. "It was so weird, Thao. I had a funny feeling that Bertha Jane was involved somehow."

"Like an angel."

"I don't know. But just there, just involved. I don't know how to explain it."

"Can't explain everything, Jason. So much we don't know about."

"I guess so."

"But things going good for you now?"

"Much better. How about you?"

"Well, I see Li a lot."

Couldn't anything stay good in my life? Even for a day? I felt like I'd been stabbed.

"Jason?"

"So are you going with him?" I finally asked, trying to stay cool.

"We just go to his house or my house."

"I mean, is he your boyfriend?" I gritted my teeth.

Thao laughed. "Not yet. Not exactly, but he is nice guy."

"I have to get off the phone, now," I said like I was in a big hurry and then I hung up, not waiting to say good-bye.

I put a CD in my Discman and listened to some music, getting totally bummed out, wishing Thao were here, wishing that she'd never moved and never met this Nice Guy, who was probably a sex maniac only she just hadn't found out yet. The whole thing was beginning to get me very depressed, so to cheer myself up, I took out my wallet and looked at Allison Gray's picture, reminding myself that at least there was one fun girl in my life, even if she was from cyberspace. But before I went to my computer to E-mail her, I went up to the kitchen to get something to eat.

I poked my head around the corner and saw Doreen loading the dishwasher. I'd been pretty successful at avoiding her since Fred got locked up and I didn't want to break my record, so I started to go back down to my room, but she heard me.

"Jason?"

"Yeah."

"There's some cold chicken from lunch, if you're hungry."

"Thanks. Maybe later." I headed back downstairs.

"Jason?"

"Yeah."

"Let me know if you need anything. I mean, if there's anything I can pick up for you when I go to the store . . . or anything."

"Okay, thanks."

I turned on my computer and then I scrounged around my desk for something to eat. I thought I had a candy bar or something, but the only thing I found was a pack of Juicy Fruit, so I chewed a piece to hold me over until Doreen was out of the kitchen.

Why couldn't she say she was sorry about locking Fred up?

Oh, screw it. I don't want to go there. I want to go to cyberspace. I chomped away on my gum and E-mailed Allison.

To: Surfsup10
From: JayKae
Subject: J. O. B.
Hi Allison,
Well I got myself a Jay Oh Bee which gets my dad off my back. This is
1 good thing, believe me. The job's cool for a job. I can bring my dog
Fred to work with me. I work for a church. This week I'm painting
some scenery for a play they're having there. Don't know when we can
IM since the hours I'm home have changed. But we can still E-mail.
Peace,

Jason

Now that Thao was involved with Nice Guy I looked forward to E-mailing Allison Gray even more. And at least I had my job, somehow that made it easier to handle the fact that Thao had a relationship with someone. My job also gave me more of a life which meant I actually had something to write about in E-mails instead of borrowing things from another person's life. It had been fun painting the scenery and I found myself getting curious to see the play, even though it was probably from the Bible with people in sheet costumes like shepherds or something. Reverend Susie was now referring to me as to the set designer, and I liked that a lot.

On Sunday afternoon, after the Samoan Christians were through, we put the finishing touches on the scenery and were carrying it up to the sanctuary.

"Do the actors read from the Bible?" I lifted my end of the butcher paper up against the back wall of the church.

"No, our play's called *The Magic Ride of Fred the Slug.*"

"Fred?"

"It was written before I met your Fred. There's also a character named Ethel who's a crow. Fred and Ethel were the names of the couple that lived upstairs from Lucy and Desi in *I Love Lucy,* but that was before your time."

"I've seen that on Nickelodeon."

"They show a lot of reruns, don't they?"

"Yeah. Did you mean a slug, like a garden slug?"

Reverend Susie nodded. "Right, he's a slimy little guy with antennae. And Ethel's an ordinary crow. The play's about how friendship endures when their hopes for glory are crushed."

"I thought the scenery was water from the Bible."

"Oh, like the Sea of Galilee or the Red Sea."

"Slugs don't swim, do they?"

"Not really. There's an otter in the play that pops up out of the water." Reverend Susie put down her end of the scenery. "Where did I put those thumbtacks?" She sighed. "I've got to go back to the office. If you want, you can read the script while I look for the thumbtacks. There's a copy on the piano."

"Okay." I got the script and sat in the first pew and read it. (I couldn't believe I was getting paid for doing this.)

The play was about a slug and a crow and how people hate them. The people love an sea otter because it is an endangered species, and Fred and Ethel want to be loved like that. Ethel gives Fred a ride on her back and they fly in front of a TV camera filming the return of the sea otter, hoping to be noticed and get famous. But the people think they look ridiculous and they still hate them. Then Fred and Ethel realize they can fly around and have fun and enjoy each other no matter what the people think.

That was about it. It was fun to read. Fred sings a little song that goes, "I'm just sliding in my slime, having an oozy-doozy time. Going icky-bicky, slicky-sloop, in my fine and fancy goop." It seemed like a good play, especially for kids, but I didn't see what was religious about it. Reverend Susie came back with the thumbtacks and I decided to ask her.

"I'll hold it down here while you put your corner up first."

I climbed up the ladder, holding on to the scenery. "Reverend Susie?"

"Ready for the tacks?"

"At least two or three." I reached down from the ladder and got the tacks from her.

"I think we should be generous with the tape, too, Jason. We wouldn't want the scenery to fall down in the middle of the play."

"Okay." I tore off a big piece of the masking tape. "I finished reading it."

"Did you like it?"

"I thought it was good."

"It's an intergenerational play. We have both adults and kids taking part." She looked up. "I need more tape on the bottom here."

I passed the tape back down to her.

"No offense, but exactly what's religious about it?"

"Maybe I should ask you what you think of as religious?"

"Prayers maybe. Stuff about God."

"Religion is actually defined as any system of beliefs or worship or conduct that involves a code of ethics and a philosophy." Reverend

Susie walked to the back of the church. "The waves show up really well, Jason. I think you've done a great job."

"Think it needs more tape?"

"Maybe one more piece for good luck."

I climbed down the ladder and got the tape that was on the floor. "What kind of principles does your religion have?" I asked her this because I still didn't see how the play was religious. "Do you have any regular prayers and stuff that you say?"

"Every service we say something together. It goes, 'Love is our doctrine, The Search for Truth is our covenant, And service is our prayer.'" She paused. "That means service to other people. Then it goes, 'To dwell together in peace, To seek knowledge in freedom, To act with courage upon our conviction, And to offer our friendship, That all souls shall come into harmony, Thus do we covenant with one another.' That's the only prayer we have."

"It seems like enough."

"We better get back to the office and start on the order of service."

"What's that?"

"It's like the program. They need to be folded in half."

When we got to the office, Reverend Susie cleared a space on the table for folding them, and while she was doing that I looked at the order of service. This phrase jumped out at me from the prayer-type thing she had just told me about, the Unison Affirmation. I freaked where it said, "The Search for Truth is our covenant," because here I was, someone who had searched for lies to send to Allison Gray and recently I'd just sent her a king-size lie, the photo of Josh and saying it was me. I got a knot in my stomach the minute I read that truth thing.

Reverend Susie divided the pile in half and we each started folding. She did three to every one of mine.

"I'm pretty slow," I mumbled.

"I've been doing this for years, you're doing fine. Everybody has a different pace." She took a stack that was folded and pushed it toward the back of the table. "It'd be boring if everyone was the same."

"But sometimes people aren't how you think they are."

"Sometimes you get fooled."

The knot got worse and I couldn't believe what happened next. All of a sudden I told her about Allison Gray. It came blurting out, like something that couldn't be stopped, like a burst pipe.

Reverend Susie just kept on folding, she didn't even look up. "Ever hear of Cyrano de Bergerac?"

"I don't think so."

"He had a funny nose and he thought he was unattractive. Now I don't think you're unattractive at all, really nice-looking I'd say, but the point of the story is that this guy thought he was unattractive. So he had a handsome friend be his stand-in to woo a woman he loved. But Cyrano wrote beautiful letters and it was his personality she fell in love with, not the handsome guy's looks, and in the end the woman was smart enough to realize that it was really Cyrano she loved. Because of his beautiful soul."

"I rented a movie like that with Steve Martin. It was called *Roxanne.*"

"Probably based on Cyrano."

"You're saying I should tell Allison the truth?"

"It's only something to think about, that's all."

I couldn't quite believe that I was talking to someone who not only didn't give me a bad time about what I'd told her, but she also didn't tell me what I should do, how I should act, who I should be.

Reverend Susie finished folding her pile and then looked at her watch. "I've got a ton of things yet to do before the service."

"I'll be done folding in a minute, then I can help."

"Good. I need some branches for the people who are playing the parts of trees. Think you could cut some for me?"

"We have a scraggy tree behind our garage where I could get some."

"You're sure it'll be okay? Because I was going to get some from my yard."

"No one sees this tree, it'll be fine."

"Great. Could you be back a little after four?"

"Sure."

"Oh, and put these by the door to the sanctuary on your way out." She handed me all the stuff we'd folded.

I left the office, and as I put them on the table by the door, I looked at a poster on the bulletin board next to the door. It was a kids' poster with a list of seven things titled "Our U.U. Principles."

1. That each and every person is important.
2. That all people should be treated fairly.
3. That our churches are places where all people are accepted and where we keep on learning together.
4. That each person must be free to search for what is true and right in life.
5. That everyone should have a vote about things that concern them.
6. That we believe in working for a peaceful, fair, and free world.
7. That we believe in caring for our planet earth.

Next to that was another poster that said, "The living tradition we share draws from many sources—wisdom from the world's religions, which inspires us in our ethical and spiritual life, and Jewish and Christian teachings, which call us to respond to God's love by loving our neighbors as ourselves."

This was the first thing I saw there that said God. I guess it was a regular religion. There was also a poster that said:

Did You Know the Following People
Were Unitarians and Universalists?

Clara Barton, Florence Nightingale, Ralph Waldo Emerson, Margaret Fuller, Whitney Young, Adlai Stevenson, Henry David Thoreau, Charles Darwin, Beatrix Potter, Susan B. Anthony, Francis Harper Watkins, Carl Sandburg, May Sarton, Kurt Vonnegut, Charles Ives, and Malvina Reynolds.

I didn't know who some of these people were, but I'd heard of a few of them, like Florence Nightingale, and I was sure the rest were important and wouldn't have gotten mixed up with something stupid.

When I got home, I had plenty of time to cut the branches before I went back to church, so I ran down to check my E-mail and Allison was there!

To: JayKae
From: Surfsup10
Subject: J. O. B
Hi Jason,
Congratulations on your Jay Oh Bee. What kind of a church is it? It sounds sort of strange that they let you bring your dog. Is it a church for dogs? I saw something on TV about pet therapists and pet cemeteries, too, so maybe they have pet churches. Do the dogs howl the hymns? Guess u cud put up with n e job as long as the pay is good. Show me the money! Right! Wassup with the girl u took to that dance? Not that I'm the jealous type!
Stay cool, later—
Allison

Maybe this jealous thing was the right strategy. I decided to play it up a little when I E-mailed back to her. I'd have to admit, I just hadn't quite gotten My Search for Truth up and running yet.

To: Surfsup10
From: JayKae
Subject: Life
Hi Allison,
Great to get ur E-mail. Karen and I rented a video last night, we're into old classics. We saw "Rear Window." We both really like old Hitchcock.

(Then I decided to write her some true stuff. Sort of a combination of true and false.)

The church where I work isn't for pets. It's a real church. The name of the play that I'm designing the set for is "The Magic Ride of Fred the Slug." The church believes in wisdom from the world's religions which inspires us in ethical and spiritual life and Jewish and Christian teachings which call us to respond to God's love by loving our neighbors as ourselves. But I saw that thing on CNN about the pet therapists. Weird.

Happy surfin'
Peace,
Jason

I shut off the machine, wishing I really had been watching videos with a girl last night, with a real girl like Thao.

Twelve

THE LATE-AFTERNOON SUN STREAMED in through the door of the garage, showing a clean, organized space, a testimony to my dad's belief in order. "A place for everything and everything in its place" was his motto. Tidiness was not one of my core values, as evidenced by the continual state of chaos in my room, but that was a battle Dad had long ago chosen to forgo, probably deciding I was hopeless.

The tools were carefully hung on a Peg-Board on the back wall, and the sun gleamed against the blades of various saws, hammers, screwdrivers, wrenches, and fancy tools whose names I didn't even know. But across the top of the Peg-Board, attached to a vinyl-handled hammer, was a magnificent spiderweb sparkling in the sunlight. *Go to it, spider! Great web! Keep going, decorate the whole board!*

I surveyed the various saws. Not knowing the difference between them . . . *eenie, meenie, minee, moe* . . . I chose a shiny one hanging on the top row. I thought I should cut branches that weren't too heavy, since the people who were the trees had to hold them through the whole play. Probably some long leafy branches would be good, but the lighter the better.

I grabbed the saw, cheered the spider some more, and went out to the apple tree next to the garage. Almost any of the lower branches seemed like they would do, so I began sawing away. I had cut off three and was starting on the fourth when I heard the kitchen door slam. I looked up to see Dad coming out carrying his golf clubs.

"Jason, what are you doing to the tree?"

"Cutting branches."

"Why?"

"Because I need them for—"

"Oh, never mind, just come over here. I want to talk to you."

Dad set his clubs down and leaned them against the car. I thought they stunk a little from Fred's pee, although I couldn't tell for sure. Then he went toward the front of the house and stood under the open window of Josh's room. "Josh, can you come down here a minute?"

Josh stuck his head out the window. "What?"

"Can you hear me from up there?"

"Yeah." Josh leaned farther out the window.

So can the whole neighborhood. "Dad . . . I've got to—"

"Wait, Jason. This won't take long." Then he yelled up to Josh. "Just stay there a minute, I want you to witness this."

"Witness what?" Josh grabbed the window handles like he wanted to close it.

"My conversation with Jason so he can't pretend he doesn't remember."

Josh began to close the window. "I don't think I want—"

"It'll just take a second." Dad turned to me, his voice even louder, and spoke slowly, enunciating each word as if he were speaking to someone comatose on the verge of being brain-dead. "Jason . . . we . . . are . . . going . . . to . . . have . . . a . . . family . . . dinner . . . tonight.   I . . . want . . . you . . . to . . . be . . . here . . . at . . . *six o'clock* . . . sharp. This is very important to Doreen. She is at the grocery story now getting all the food." Dad looked up at Josh. "Now he can't say he wasn't told, right?"

"I can't come." I looked at my watch.

"What d'ya mean you can't come!"

"I've got to cut more branches. I have to go to church."

"What the hell are you talking about? Branches for church!"

"It's for a play they're having. *The Magic Ride of Fred the Slug*."

"Jesus Christ. Have you gotten yourself mixed up with some kind of cult!"

"It's not a cult!" I screamed at him.

"Only losers get in these cults," Dad screams back. "Wackos and creeps! Are you crazy, Jason!"

Then Josh leans out the window. "SHUT UP!"

Dad and I stare up at him. Josh leans out the window so far it looks like he might fall out if he had regular legs instead of the tree trunks he walks around on.

"There's nothing wrong with Jason!" he screams at Dad. "Do you know how many wasted people there are out there? At least he's not a druggie!"

Then he slammed the window down so hard a pane popped and flew down and crashed on the driveway.

I stared at the shattered glass that was all over the asphalt. Then I stared up at Josh's room, but he was gone. I looked at Dad, but he had turned away from me. Slowly, like a robot, he walked to his car, opened the trunk, hoisted up his golf clubs, and shoved them in. I watched him as he shut the trunk and got in the car. He looked over his shoulder at the street as he backed out of the drive. Then he was gone. He never looked back.

I went inside for a broom and the dustpan, then went back out and swept up the driveway, realizing this was the second time since Josh and Doreen had moved in that I was sweeping up broken glass. As the dustpan filled with the glass splinters, I glanced up at Josh's window and tried to think of a time when someone had stood up for me before, but I couldn't remember it ever happening. Not even once—and that really got me.

I looked at my watch. I'd have to finish cutting that last branch, then load them in my car and leave pretty soon. But I didn't want to leave without talking to Josh. I went as fast as I could on that last branch, sawing like a guy in a logging derby, then ran to my car, heaved them in the trunk, and went in to find him.

Josh was downstairs in the den, slumped in a chair in front of the TV. But he didn't seem to be watching anything, just surfing the channels.

"Josh?"

"Yeah." He stared at the TV, not looking up.

"Thanks."

"For what?"

"Taking my side."

"I call 'em like I see 'em."

"Yeah. Well, thanks anyway."

Josh put the TV on mute. "You know what really gets me? It's the way they think they can make an instant family, and we're not even going to blink."

"I know."

"Do you? I'll tell you something, Jason. I get sick of having to be this great hoop man. It's like my parents expect it and nothing less. They can jack me around but it's no big thing to them because they're sure I'll make it anywhere I go because of basketball. Like moving here in my senior year. It stinks." He clicked off the TV and threw the remote on the couch. "I've always wondered if they'd pay any attention to me if I were just a regular kid, but I've always been afraid to find out. I envy you, Jason."

"You're being sarcastic, of course."

"No. I'm serious."

"I'm a crappy athlete, I don't have a girlfriend, and if I told you what I really like to do you'd really think I was weird."

"Try me."

"Okay. What the hell. What I really like to do is feed birds. I feed birds, Josh."

Josh stared at me.

"Weird, see. I told you."

"I don't care if you feed birds or squirrels or whatever. You've got friends. I bet you and Kenny have hung around forever."

"Since first grade."

"I can't remember the names of anyone I knew in elementary school. And I finally figured out that there wasn't much point in getting too tight with anyone because we'd just have to move anyway."

"But everywhere you go you get a girl."

"I'm not whining about that. But I'll tell you, it's the same thing like with my parents. I really wonder sometimes if it weren't for the basketball if they'd give me the time of day."

I looked at my watch. "Oh man, I gotta go." I started to leave, but then I stopped. "You want to come with me?"

"Where?"

"Church?"

"I'll pass. But thanks."

"Okay, see ya."

"Jason?"

"Yeah?"

"It must be nice to feed birds. I mean to do something you like and it doesn't matter if you win or if anyone watches."

I still wondered if he actually thought it was hilarious and was putting me on, and I waited for him to break out laughing. But he didn't—it seemed like he really meant it.

"You're right. You can't lose at bird feeding."

"Yeah, can't be off your game."

"Hey, are you gonna be here later tonight? There's something I want to talk to you about."

"Sure."

"Okay. Later."

By the time I got to church, most of the actors had arrived and were in a room off to the side of the pulpit getting in their costumes. I brought in the branches for the people who were going to be trees, and Reverend Susie introduced me to everyone as her new assistant. After I'd given the actors the branches there wasn't anything for me to do, so I went in the sanctuary and sat in one of the pews in the back. Not long after I sat down, a guy with a beard and a ponytail came down the aisle putting books on all the seats. "These are the ones we use," he said, handing me a charcoal gray book. "The red book in the slot in the pew in front of you belongs to the Fletcher Street Congregationalists and the Samoan Christians, and the black book, *Sabbath and Festival Prayer Book*, is used by Temple Emmanuel. We keep ours in the back and just hand them out at each service."

I looked at the book the guy handed me, *Singing the Living Tradition.* Then I looked at the books in the slot in the pew in front of me and thought it was kind of interesting how each group of people had a different idea of what songs to sing or what words to say, so they each needed their own book.

The guy with the ponytail had finished distributing the books and was walking back down the center aisle. He didn't look like my idea of a churchgoer in his jeans and sweatshirt. Then people started coming in and I noticed they were also dressed really casual too, most of them in jeans. I wasn't sure what I had expected. Reverend Susie had told me I didn't need to dress up, but I thought she just meant because I was bringing the branches.

As I looked around, I realized that I had no memory of actually being in church before. It's possible that I could have been, maybe in a church or even a synagogue for that matter, because of the backgrounds of my parents. But I had to have been really young, since I couldn't remember. But I still had an image in my mind of church from movies and weddings and funerals on TV, and I thought people would be dressed up. The guys in suits, and the women in dresses and everyone would be quiet. But as more and more people came in, there were only a few who were dressed up. Most of them looked like they could just as easily be going bowling or to a basketball game, and they weren't quiet or hushed up at all as they greeted each other and found seats.

A few minutes after five, the service started. I followed along the program and basically copied what everyone did. I liked standing up and singing a song from the book together with the other people. It was nice to be doing something with a bunch of other people even though I didn't know them. And the music they had was good; two women with great voices sang a Paul Simon song and it really got me.

Then the play started and it was funny and the scenery I made looked fine and didn't fall down. Most of all it was awesome to hear Reverend Susie get up there in the pulpit and give her endangerment sermon. The main idea seemed to be that children living in poverty are an endangered species. Her voice was different from when you just talked to her, it was powerful and commanding, but at the same time gentle. Most of the people seemed to be really listening except for one little kid whose parents had to take her out and a guy who snored.

And the people were friendly at the potluck. Reverend Susie announced again that I was her new assistant and it seemed like almost everyone made it a point to welcome me. While I was getting a second helping of tuna casserole, one of the women in the choir came up. "It's great you're working with Reverend Susie. We had heard all about you from Bertha Jane."

"Really?"

"Oh, sure. And Thao, too." She heaped some salad on her plate. "Do you know how she's doing?"

"Pretty well, I guess. We write and I call her sometimes."

"We'd love to see her again. We all became so attached to her through Bertha Jane."

Then someone clinked a spoon against a glass to get attention and a number of people stood up and made announcements. Things like volunteering for the schools, an emergency feeding program for homeless people, and cleaning up a rose garden on Rainier Avenue. I looked around and listened to the things they were doing and I couldn't say if these people were really nicer on a day-to-day basis than any other bunch of people, but they did seem be trying to do some good for the world. And they knew Bertha Jane and Thao. I also liked the tuna casserole and as I scarfed it down, it hit me that I felt more at home here than in my own house.

The peaceful feeling I had lasted until I got home. It was almost like I had gotten a little high on being at church, like I was filled with warm sugar or something. But it wasn't just church, it was from talking to Josh. I couldn't get over the fact that he had stood up for me. And although I knew I still wasn't brave enough to tell Josh I had sent his picture to Allison Gray, one thing had changed.

While I was at church I had said the Unison Affirmation with all the people. I started out okay saying, "Love is our doctrine," but then I started to gag when I said the next line, the one about the search for truth. I actually had this coughing fit and could hardly say the line that came after that, "And service is our prayer." I was about to leave the place to get some water when the coughing finally stopped, and right then and there I decided I didn't want to keep pretending with Allison Gray. It was bad for my health.

I also remembered the play Reverend Susie had told me about that was like that Steve Martin movie. How the woman discovered the guy who had been writing her wasn't the handsome dude, but she loved him anyway for his beautiful soul. I didn't think I had a beautiful soul, but I wasn't mad at everything the way I'd been after Bertha Jane died. In fact, I felt better than I had since my mom first moved out—and I wanted to tell Allison Gray who I really was.

I went to my computer and turned it on. I waited to get on-line, wondering how I was going to tell her.

To: Surfsup10
From: JayKae
Subject: pic

Hey Allison, I made a little mistake and sent the wrong picture. Sorry.

This was a lot harder than I thought. I stared at the screen some more and then started typing.

To: Surfsup10
From: JayKae
Subject: pic

Allison, my picture wasn't ready so I sent my stepbrother's instead. lol.
Pretty funny ha!

Delete! This was getting impossible. But then I thought again about the movie and decided to write the truth. After all, now things were going a lot better in my life and maybe I was on some kind of a roll.

Hi Allison,
I really like my new job. And it's probably because of the minister at this church where I work and all that I decided that I had to tell you the truth about me. I'm not the guy in the picture. That was my step-brother, Josh Kemple. He really does look like Leo and he's a big bas-ketball star. I don't think there's much special about me. I'm average looking, I do average in school. And the car I drive is below average. I like all animals, especially dogs. I have a great dog named Fred. That's about it. The stuff I wrote you about the kind of music I like is true. And it's true that my dad got married. I hope after learning this that you will still want to stay in touch with me. I really had fun getting your IM's.
Peace,
Jason Kovak
P.S. I'm attaching my real pic. It was taken at my dad's wedding. All that stuff was also true, about the wedding.

I read it over about three times with my hand poised on the mouse, ready to click it on "send," and waited to get up the nerve. I thought about Bertha Jane. What would she tell me to do? *Easy.* I hit "send."

▱ Thirteen

Reverend Susie wanted me to get an extra person to help move a desk and some bookcases to the church that somebody had donated. She said they were big and old and pretty heavy, but she was excited about having them. I asked Kenny if he wanted the job and he did, he even said we could use his uncle's van. We had arranged to pick the stuff up after school and met at our lockers after the last bell so we could leave together. On our way to the parking lot, when we passed the gym, I stopped for a second and looked in at the basketball team. "I want to watch Josh a minute," I said.

"Okay, I'll get the van and bring it around. Meet you by the door."

Kenny had a new girlfriend now, Gretchen Coe, and I don't think he had it in for Josh the way he had around the time of the Kimberly Cotton thing. Although I wouldn't say he was Josh's biggest fan either.

I watched Josh for a few minutes and waved when he glanced

up and saw me. They were practicing free throws and I gave him a thumbs-up after he sank his, then I left to meet Kenny.

"Hey, Jason! Wait a second." He trotted over to the door. "When do you get home tonight?"

"I'll probably get a bite to eat at work, so it'll be around seven I guess. Why?"

"This morning your dad gave me a ride and said he wanted us to fix the window."

"Good."

"Good?"

"That he's not just blaming you for breaking it."

"Well, the thing is . . . I'm not much of a handyman."

"Me either."

The whistle blew and Josh had to leave. I was kind of glad he said he wasn't much of a handyman so we'd be equally unskilled at fixing the window. Maybe Dad would be more patient showing us what to do when he found out Josh wasn't exactly ready to star on *This Old House.*

I went out to the parking lot just as Kenny drove up in the van. I didn't say anything about Josh; it still seemed better not to say much. Instead we talked about the Sonics, stuff he'd seen on the Net, all the usual stuff. And luckily, the traffic wasn't that bad so we made it down to the south end and got to the church in about twenty-five minutes.

When we pulled up, Reverend Susie was waiting for us with the address of the house where we were supposed to get the furniture. I introduced her to Kenny and she stuck her hand in the window and shook hands.

"It's great to have your van. The desk is huge, I'm afraid you might have to make two trips."

"No problem, we're the dynamic duo, right, Jason?"

"Got that right."

We left the church and drove over to Seward Park Avenue. But then Kenny stopped and pulled over. "I think I ought to check a map. See if there's one, will you?"

I opened the glove compartment and pulled out a Seattle map. "Here's one."

"Good. I think we go south here, but I'm not sure." Kenny unfolded the map and then checked the address again. "She seems nice."

"Reverend Susie?"

"Yeah." Kenny folded the map up and handed it back to me. "She doesn't seem like a minister."

"I know, sometimes she seems a little out there."

"Like how?"

"She says stuff like 'serendipity' a lot and her church put on a play about a crow and a slug."

Kenny turned south on Seward Park Avenue. "I remember when you first went to work for Bertha Jane and thought she was a nutcase."

"I know. But I changed my mind."

Moving the furniture didn't take very long at all, and after we had taken the desk and both bookcases in the church, Kenny drove me home so I could get Fred and get back to work. Reverend Susie wanted me to enter the names and addresses of the newcomers on the computer and bring the database up to date.

When I got home Doreen's car was in the drive but she wasn't downstairs, which was fine with me. I was in a hurry to get Fred and get out of there. I was also getting my Discman because when I do that stuff on the computer, I like to listen to music. I was leafing through my CDs when I heard a knock on the door.

"Jason?"

"Yeah?"

"Can I come in?" Doreen cautiously poked her head around the door.

"Sure. But I'm about to leave for work."

"This won't take long."

"Okay."

Doreen came in but stayed by the door. "All I came to say was that Josh told me about how you guys have been feeling."

"He did?"

"Yes. He said both of you resented the way your dad and I tried to make us into a family so fast."

"Well . . . moving here wasn't that easy for him."

She nodded. "I know, and he told me I shouldn't have painted your house and changed everything."

I wondered if I looked as shocked as I felt.

"Jack and I are going to try to be more understanding, that's all I can say, except that I'm sorry if I've made it harder for you."

"Why doesn't Dad talk to me himself?"

"I don't know. I really don't. I don't think he had much of a relationship with his father—"

"So that's why he won't talk to me? What's that got to do with it?"

"Sometimes I think maybe he just doesn't know how to act."

"It would help if he'd get off my case."

"I think Josh got through to him, Jason, and I think he's going to try. And that's all we can ask, isn't it really? That a person tries?"

I looked at Doreen and her face seemed puffier than usual, maybe from crying. And then it seemed like Bertha Jane was there, I could almost feel her drawing me toward Doreen and then Doreen was hugging me and it stunk like gardenias, and I was hugging her back.

When I got back from work, Josh and Dad were in the kitchen waiting for me. It was the first time I'd seen Dad since yesterday afternoon when the window broke. He seemed really uncomfortable, nothing like his usual barking, blustery self, which surprised me since it was close to seven-thirty.

"Sorry I'm home a little later than I thought."

"No problem by me," Josh said.

I waited, expecting Dad would gather some momentum, regain

his focus, and yell at me for not being there at seven. *Jason, why can't you ever get it right!*

But he didn't say anything. He'd start to look me in the eye and then he'd look away. I guess maybe if he's not yelling at me he really doesn't know how to act. It's like he could use a set of directions or something. Or a book like *How to Relate to Your Son if You're Not Lecturing or Yelling at Him: One Hundred Phrases for Any and Every Occasion.*

"Josh said you wanted us to fix the window tonight?"

Reminding him of this seemed to get him unstuck. "Right. Now the first thing you guys should do is measure the window. Then you can go to Eagle Hardware and order the glass to fit. After that I'll show you how to put it in."

Dad handed me the tape measure. "Measure the glass itself, and when you're at Eagle be sure and pick up some new putty. Just tell them what you're doing and they'll give you what you need. We have a putty knife so don't bother with that."

"Okay." This time Dad looked at me as I took the tape measure, and it seemed like his eyes were trying to talk, like an alien trying to make contact with a creature he had never seen before and didn't know the language.

I followed Josh up the stairs to his room and when we got to the landing where the stairs turned, I realized that I hadn't been in his room since he'd moved in. Not that he'd been down to my room, either. It was pretty clear we both hadn't wanted much to do with each other. His room, which had been our old guest room, hadn't been painted, but the walls were covered now with all his posters, which were all from the NBA, mostly Chicago Bulls and Michael Jordan. The top of the dresser was filled with plaques and trophies, and on the table by his bed there was a picture in a silver frame of his girlfriend from Chicago.

"She's really pretty."

"It was hard to leave."

"What about you and Kimberly?"

"She's fun. I don't know, I'm not going to be here that long."

"You sure don't have a problem with the ladies." I went over to the window and pulled out the tape measure. "You're an expert."

"Whatever success I have I owe it to Gramps." Josh held the end of the tape in place while I pulled it out.

"Looks like it's twenty-four across. Think we should write it down?"

"Wouldn't hurt." Josh went to his desk and looked for a piece of paper.

"So who's Gramps? Your grandfather?"

"Yeah. Gramps and Gran, my dad's parents. I stayed with them a lot."

"In Chicago?"

"Near there, in Evanston. But they're both dead now."

"That's too bad."

"They were pretty old."

"I know, but it's still sad."

Josh was quiet for a minute. Then he smiled. "My grandfather was this great guy. One time when I was about twelve I was staying there and a girl called up to talk to me and I freaked out. I didn't know what to say, so I told Gramps to tell her I wasn't there."

"It's kind of hard to picture that."

"What?"

"You freaking out."

"Well . . . I hid or something so he told her I'd be back soon. He said he was sure I'd like to talk to her and he got her number."

"You didn't mind him messing in your business?"

"No, he was great. Then he told me that there were three things to remember about women. He said they were true no matter what age I was and if I knew these three things I would always be successful with them."

"Get another piece of paper. I want to write this down."

"You'll remember, it's easy. He said, 'Number One: Tell them they're pretty. Number Two: Don't yell at them, and Number Three: Always leave the toilet seat down.'"

"It can't be that easy."

"Maybe. But I don't think it's as stupid as it sounds. He also added a fourth. 'Just for good measure,' he said. The fourth thing would be—don't spit on the sidewalk."

"I never have learned to do that."

"What?"

"Spit. In middle school I remember trying, but I just spit on my shoe."

"Me, too." Josh laughed. "On my pants."

I wanted to talk to Josh about Thao. I'd been wondering if I should just fold my tent and back off when it came to her. Maybe I just had to deal with it and accept the fact that any hope of having more than a friendship with Thao was over now that she was seeing this other guy. But it's hard for a guy to ask another guy for advice, we're always supposed to have an image like we know everything and not show any weakness to another guy. And not asking for help was pretty ingrained in me. I finally made up my mind to ask him for advice when we were in the car on our way to Eagle Hardware, but instead I choked and never said a word.

At the store, I told myself I'd try again. I'd casually mention it while the guy cut the glass for us, or while we got the putty, or while we were at the cash register, but again I choked. When I got in the car after we put the glass in the trunk, the conversation in my head really got going.

You'll be sorry if you don't talk about it.

But he'll think I'm lame.

He already knows you feed birds.

This is different.

Why?

Because it is! Not knowing about girls is just different than feeding birds.

He knows you don't have a girlfriend. Just ask him. There's nothing to lose.

The logic of this last argument seemed to click in, and as we waited at the light on McClellan I took the plunge, trying all the while to sound extremely casual. "I wanted to ask you something, Josh." I said as I adjusted the rearview mirror.

"Sure."

"About a girl I know."

"Someone at school?"

"No. She lives in California, she's a friend. We both used to work for the same old lady. In fact the church where I work sponsored her to come here from Vietnam and my boss, Reverend Susie, knows her. She had to move when the old lady died."

"You know what I think about moving."

"Yeah." I hesitated for a minute, then braced myself and forged ahead. "The problem is, I want to be more than friends, but she's starting to see this other guy and I don't know what to do about it."

"If there's one thing I know about, it's long-distance relationships. They don't last long if you don't see the person, believe me."

"But what about the other guy?"

"Just 'cause the other team shows up, you don't quit the game."

"I'm not much of a jock."

"Doesn't matter, look at it this way. You go to feed birds and you never know if they'll show up."

"I guess so."

"I mean, you make the effort, right? Even though there's no guarantee what'll happen. So with a girl, first off you have to see her and spend time together, be together in real time. I was looking in the paper at air fares because I want to get back to Chicago for a long weekend . . . The fares between here and California are cheap."

"It would be too weird for me to visit her. She lives with her aunt and I'm pretty sure they only want her to be with a guy who's Vietnamese."

"So send her a ticket and have her come up here to visit."

"What about her family?"

"See, it's really her problem about how to deal with her family, and they'll have to deal with the fact that things are different here, people meet each other and they don't always stay with their own group. We're too mixed up for that so it happens. I've lived in a lot of different places and in big cities anyway, you see everybody with everybody."

"She might not want to, now that she's seeing this guy."

"You never know unless you take your shot."

"I don't know if they'd let her come, though."

"Couldn't she stay with your boss? I mean, why not ask? All anyone can say is 'no.' "

"Man, that's brilliant."

If Reverend Susie went along with this, there might be a chance!

I wanted to hug Josh. I wanted to jump in the air and high-five and then punch his shoulder and bump heads and do all that stuff athletes do on TV when a guy scores a goal or a touchdown or makes the free throw that wins the game.

After we got the window fixed I went down to check my E-mail. As great as it was talking to Josh about Thao, the Allison Gray thing was more my private fantasy and I didn't want him knowing about her. Even though I'd ended up telling Allison the truth, this cyber-relationship was something I definitely wanted to keep secret.

When I turned on the computer and put in my password for AOL, there was the little yellow envelope and the guy said, "You have mail."

All right! There it was . . . an E-mail from Surfsup10! Things had been going so much better for me lately, I was sure that when I opened Allison's E-mail, I would find out that everything was okay, that she was glad I'd set it straight and it didn't matter. We'd keep on E-mailing each other and it would be great. We might even meet someday, who knows? There were so many incredible possibilities!

There were a bunch of other E-mails, too. All the usual junk stuff and I opened them and then deleted them, one by one, saving Allison's for last. (It's the same way I eat cake, I always save the frosting for last.) I got all the junk deleted and then slowly, with my eyes glued to the screen, I leaned forward and opened her message.

To: JayKae
From: Surfsup10
Subject: None

You dog. I knew you were weird when you said you worked at a
church. I hate religious freaks! Get out of my life. Don't e-mail me
again. EVER!

So much for truth. So much for my beautiful soul. I read it over
a few times, wondering what a religious freak really was. Maybe
Reverend Susie knew. The thing that was so strange, though, was
that even though I was disappointed when I read her E-mail, I wasn't
crushed. *I wasn't destroyed.* I read it one more time, then hit "delete."
The message box came on the screen: "Are you sure you want to
delete the selected letter? They cannot be recovered once deleted."

I hit "delete" again, and she was gone, Allison Gray now deleted
from my life.

The next afternoon at work, after I'd finished putting labels on
the church newsletter, Reverend Susie and I were having tea in her
office, and I told her about what had happened.

"You know that girl I told you about. The one I E-mailed?"

"The girl from Hawaii?"

"Right. Well, I told her the truth about me and she went nuts.
She didn't go for my beautiful soul."

"Well, it's her loss. Because you have one."

"She said because I work for a church I was a religious freak."

"I'll tell you something, just mentioning religion can make people uncomfortable. We have so many religions, our country would
fall apart if we didn't respect a person's right to believe what they
want. Or a person's right not to believe, for that matter." Reverend
Susie smiled. "The conventional wisdom says it's best not to discuss
religion, sex, and politics, so we can avoid controversy and preserve
harmony."

Speaking of sex, Reverend Susie. I would like to have some.

I sipped my tea and watched Reverend Susie pat Fred, but I didn't say what had just popped into my head. It was easier to talk about harmony. "Things are better at home," I told her.

"That's great."

"My stepbrother is okay. We're starting to get along, at least everybody seems to be trying."

"Can't ask any more than that."

"That's what my stepmother said."

"Well, I agree with her. Sounds like she'll be okay. Stepparents don't have it easy, you know. They fall in love and then get someone else's children in their lives who resent them a lot of times. It's almost a miracle when it works out." She looked out the window. "Maybe love is always a miracle."

Reverend Susie sounded so much like Bertha Jane it made me feel embarrassed about the thoughts about sex that are always popping into my brain. I remembered again the time Bertha Jane said, "I'm not against sex, Jason, but sometimes when things are felt with lust and passion, true friendship can be obscured."

But being so attracted to Thao had never messed up my friendship with her, and I knew that if what I wanted didn't work out, I could always count on our friendship. I knew, too, there was no one in my life easier to talk to than Reverend Susie and I had to ask her before I lost my nerve and wimped out.

"I used to think it would be a miracle if I ever saw Thao again. But then my stepbrother told me that plane fares aren't that much to California." I looked at Reverend Susie as she scratched Fred's ears and I thought about what Josh had said. *All anyone can say is 'no.'*

"Reverend Susie? I was wondering if Thao came for a visit if she could stay with you? If you'd talk to her aunt?"

"I'd love to have her."

"You'd love to have her?"

"Sure. Have you thought about when?"

Could it actually be this easy?

"Jason?"

"Huh?"

"What dates did you have in mind?"

"Maybe spring vacation?"

"Do you know the dates?"

"The dates?"

"Of spring vacation?"

"The week of April 12th, I'm pretty sure, but I really don't know if Thao would want to come."

"I should probably clear it with her aunt first and then you and Thao can figure out if you want to go ahead." Reverend Susie went to her desk and rummaged around a bunch of papers. "All I need to do is check the calendar which is here somewhere in this mess. But as far as I know that week would be great. I talked to Nu-Anh a lot when we were arranging for Thao to leave, so I'd be happy to call her about it."

Later I wondered, are a lot of things like that? Things that seem too hard, almost impossible, but that once you finally get up the nerve aren't so hard after all?

That afternoon after work, I went to Seward Park to feed the birds. I threw a stick for Fred as we walked around the perimeter of the park next to the water. He was jumping for joy, acting just the way I felt. Because even if it turned out Thao didn't visit, just the possibility was incredible.

At the north end of the lake, I went to the bench where I always sat. There was a bronze plaque set in the concrete which held the bench. I had never paid that much attention to it before, but today I read it.

ELIJAH AARON REED

1992

A GENTLE INSPIRATION TO HIS MANY FRIENDS

Friends. I thought about Josh and I realized that I'd never be the kind of person who could get excited about the Beasley Motivation

Seminar, and Josh would probably never be interested in going to my church or feeding birds. But I knew something important. I knew we'd be friends.

I looked down at the plaque. I threw a handful of bread crumbs on the grass and within seconds the birds were there, and as I watched them hop around getting the crumbs, I thought about this guy Elijah Aaron Reed. I didn't even know him, but I knew he had what mattered in his life. He had friends.

⌂ Fourteen

I T WAS A CLEAR NIGHT as I drove to the airport. The sky was midnight blue and it looked like it had been sprayed with stars. As I drove past the Mt. Baker Community Club, I remembered the last time I was there. It was election day and there was a flag draped over the door. It was raining hard and Thao and I had stood in the rain with a sign telling people to vote for Bertha Jane. Bertha Jane's name was still on the ballot and even though she had died, Thao and I wanted to stand there for her on election day. I was surprised how long ago that seemed now.

I got more and more nervous as I drove south on I-5. What if I got weird when I saw Thao, if I didn't know how to act or what to say or do? What if I got sick and got dizzy and freaked out or threw up?

I tried to convince myself that Thao wanted to come to see me and that everything would be okay, but my heart jumped around like a grasshopper on a hot stove and I almost missed the exit to the airport.

I parked on level J, which was good because I knew I wouldn't forget the first letter of my name, although I was in such a state that anything was possible. The stall number was 64, and I couldn't think of a way to remember that except that 6 and 4 add up to 10, which made me think of Surfsup10 and I didn't want to be thinking about that disaster right now. I didn't have a pen to write it down so I just kept saying "64" to myself over and over as I took the elevator to the fourth floor, then ran across the sky bridge to the airport.

The Alaska Airlines arrival screen showed that her flight was early! I couldn't believe it. It would be here in two minutes! I ran to the gate and by the time I got through the security check and down to the gate the plane was just pulling up.

I waited with a bunch of people and after a few minutes the passengers started coming through the door. A business guy with a briefcase, an old couple with white hair, a lady carrying a baby . . . I watched each person while my heart pounded so hard I was sure it must be vibrating through the airport like the bass on a car radio turned up full blast.

Then I saw her. And she was more beautiful than I remembered. I melted as she saw me and smiled and hurried toward me and I shouldn't have worried about knowing what to do.

I took her in my arms and kissed her.

Thanks, Bertha Jane, I thought, as I held Thao and pressed my cheek against her dark hair.

Thanks for looking out for me.